Harrigan's Price
&
Other Stories

Christian Bauer

The following works have previously appeared in:

Fresh, Never Frozen — Untreed Reads (2011)

Harrigan's Price — Untreed Reads (2011)

Killer of a Deal — Untreed Reads (2011)

The Winter of Her Discontent — Untreed Reads (2012)

Special Charter — Untreed Reads (2011)

Disposal — *Blood Rose* (February 2013)

Five Stars — An earlier version, under the title of *Quality Assurance,* appeared in *From the Asylum* (July 2005)

Meggapizza — *Chaos Theory Tales Askew #9* (Fall 2006)

The When of Gadgets — *Phantasmical Contraptions* (2021)

The World of Your Dreams — An earlier version appears in *Fall into Fantasy* (2020)

Harrigan's Price
&
Other Stories
Christian Bauer

This edition published by Sandra Murphy Presents
An imprint of Misti Media LLC
https://whitecitypress.com
Available in both Paperback and eBook Editions
1 2 3 4 5 6 7 8 9 10
Copyright Respective Authors © 2024
Paperback ISBN: 9781963479348
eBook ISBN: 9781963479331

Without limiting the rights under copyright reserved above, no part of this publication may be reproduced, stored in or introduced into a retrieval system, or transmitted, in any form, or by any means (electronic, mechanical, photocopying, recording, or otherwise), without the prior written permission of both the copyright owners and the above publisher of this book.

The scanning, uploading, and distribution of this book via the Internet or via any other means without the permission of the publisher is illegal and punishable by law. Please purchase only authorized electronic editions, and do not participate in or encourage electronic piracy of copyrighted materials. Your support of the author's rights is appreciated.

Dedication

To Writers Under the Arch in St. Louis, whose critique improved these stories and to Sandra Murphy, the Goddess of Editors.

Contents

Introduction

Chris Bauer likes his stories short furnished with twists and turns readers won't see coming. Sit back and enjoy a variety of locations, plots, and an introduction to very strange people and the worlds they live in.

Fresh Never Frozen

At two o'clock in the morning of the Wednesday before Thanksgiving, the poultry truck pulled away from the dock in a cloud of autumn haze and diesel exhaust.

"First we put the fresh turkeys in the cooler," said Jeff. "The stuffing and cranberries can wait."

"Who buys a fresh turkey the day before Thanksgiving?" asked Brad.

"Enough people for you and me to work overtime," said Jeff. A big, grey-bearded Irishman, he looked like he should have been in a movie with knights and castles. He pressed the large red CLOSE button, and the loading bay door rattled down.

Brad pulled the motorized cart to the stack of boxes labeled FRIEND FARMS FRESH NEVER FROZEN. One carton inched its way off the stack.

Brad ignored what he saw. He had seen a pallet of soup cans fall over on its own and a crate of hand soap implode. If you unloaded grocery pallets long enough, you could see anything.

The box of Thanksgiving turkeys leaped off the pallet. Its companion scooted to the edge to fill its place.

Brad hesitated. "Uh, the fresh turkey ain't dead yet."

"You're supposed to be off that shit," said Jeff. He pulled a half-pint whiskey bottle from his back pocket and took a long swig.

The box exploded. Three turkeys, deathly white and ready for the oven, stood on their drumsticks. They shook off the packing ice, bent over, and ejected packets of giblets from their rumps.

"Whoa. This is weird," said Brad.

Box after the box fell on the floor and burst open to free its FRIENDS FARMS FRESH NEVER FROZEN turkeys. The dead poultry gathered in a flock, and at once, turned their headless torsos toward Brad and Jeff.

Jeff shook his head like a boxer who had fought too many rounds. He drained his whiskey bottle.

"They're fresh, but they're not dead," said Brad.

The mob of oven-ready turkeys formed a poultry phalanx, and shedding ice chips and giblet bags behind them, advanced on Brad and Jeff.

"I don't think they like us," said Brad.

"Why should they like us?" asked Jeff.

Brad and Jeff retreated, their backs against pallets of packaged stuffing and canned cranberries.

"What are they going to do to us? They're dead turkeys," said Jeff.

"I'm not going to wait and find out, "said Brad. He reached against the wall for the aluminum baseball bat officially used to break up bags of ice.

The fresh never-frozen turkeys advanced within reaching distance. Brad teed up like a hockey forward playing baseball and swung. The bat hit the fowl butterball with a wet thud, and it skittered across the floor. Two more stepped into its place.

Brad wound up again, his backswing smashing into the backstop of cardboard cartons. Dried crumbs, herbs, and bread cubes of turkey stuffing poured out.

The fresh never-frozen phalanx halted.

Brad leaned on the bat. "I scared them off."

Jeff reached across pulled a handful of stuffing from the box and threw it at the nearest bird. It wiggled back on its abbreviated legs.

"They're afraid of the stuffing," he said.

Brad thrust his fist into the box and hurled a handful. The breading shrapnel struck the nearest. It fell to the floor and laid still, and its fowl companions backed away.

"I killed one," shouted Brad.

"They're already dead," said Jeff. He measured the distance to the exit with his eyes. "We grab as much stuffing as we can and make a run for the door."

Brad filled his arms with the cellophane bags, then reconsidered. "We got to throw and carry at the same time."

They each opened a bag. "On the count of three," said Jeff.

On 'two' Brad flung fistfuls of dried turkey stuffing and Jeff followed. The safety of the door was a few yards away when the turkeys cut them off and began to close ranks behind them. Throwing stuffing side to side, Jeff and Brad made it back to their corrugated box base.

"OK," said Jeff. "We make a wall of stuffing and wait them out." He glanced at his watch. "It's two thirty. The produce truck comes at five. We have to hold out for two and a half hours."

Jeff and Brad tore open all four cardboard boxes, ripped apart plastic bags, and laid a barrier of turkey stuffing around them. The fresh never-frozen fowl phalanx reformed its ranks, and advanced. The turkeys stopped at the edge of the stuffing barrier, hesitating like soldiers at the edge of a minefield.

"See, we're good," said Jeff.

"Want to try for the door again?" asked Brad.

"We ran out of stuffing."

Brad studied the remaining boxes and grinned. "If they don't like stuffing, maybe they don't like cranberries."

Brad opened the box and pulled out a can.

"Now we gotta open it," said Jeff.

Brad brought out his Swiss Army Knife, and holding it in his fist, stabbed the top of a cranberry can. The blade folded into his fingers. He screamed, and blood joined the red cranberries. The turkeys rocked drumstick to drumstick as they shivered in anticipation like demons at the scent of fresh souls.

"Not good," said Jeff. "They smell blood and they like it."

Jeff took the pocketknife as Brad tried to staunch the blood flow with paper towels.

Jeff folded the blade closed and opened one of the knife's tools.

"What's that?" asked Brad.

"A can opener." He worked at the lid, a quarter of an inch at a time, until with his fingertips he pulled back the lid. He waved the opened can of cranberry sauce at the turkeys, and the glob of red landed among the turkeys with a splat. They scattered, then gathered out of range.

"I told you. They're turkeys," said Brad.

"They're dead turkeys that shouldn't be escaping their boxes," reminded Jeff. "I open the cans, and you spread out the cranberries."

It was slow cutting open the cans. The turkeys became bolder, poking a drumstick over the stuffing like a swimmer testing the water.

Brad and Jeff leaned against the wall.

"We're safe for now," said Brad.

"Duh," said Jeff. He pulled his cell phone from his pocket and flipped it open. His fingers hesitated over the screen. "They'll think we're drunk or stoned or both. I need this job."

Brad shook his head. "Don't look at me. I'm on probation."

Jeff pulled out his backup whiskey bottle and slouched against the pile of empty cartons. "Now we wait."

Brad yawned. "We're good. We can hold out."

"If we don't fall asleep," said Jeff.

They didn't notice the mice, sniffing and scampering, drawn by the feast of turkey stuffing and cranberries.

Harrigan's Price

"I'd sell my soul to shoot those bastards down."

Harrigan made a gun sight with his fingers and aimed high into the South Pacific night.

The sky was blacker than anything back home, dense with the diamond dust of unfamiliar stars. Three Japanese seaplane bombers passed overhead and blotted out the constellations. The faint roar of heavy aircraft engines clung to the air like the pervasive stench of the jungle.

"Selling your soul is a high price." The Chaplain took another long swallow of scotch. For a week, awake and asleep, he was pulling a young pilot out of the shot-up fighter plane. *We got a live one*, he remembered yelling.

He was wrong. The boy coughed blood and died.

On some nights, the memory suffocated like the thick, tropical air.

The deep growl of the bombers' engines faded. In a few moments would come the flashes on the horizon and the faint rumble of bombs.

"They're pounding the poor Aussies," said Harrigan.

"Port Moresby's all that's between us and the Emperor of Japan." He took another sip of scotch. "Somebody's got to do something."

The Chaplain drained his cup and took a deep breath. Mass for the Living, and Last Rites for the dying. Medical orderly. Baseball game arranger. Letter writer. Confidant. Rescue crew. Dispenser of liquor for "medicinal" purposes. He did it all, except for the killing.

The Chaplain shielded his flashlight and thumbed through a crumpled Army paperback.

"Kawanishi flying boat," he read. "Length… Wingspan… Four engines… Weight, thirty- five tons. Eight twenty- millimeter cannon. Believed to be armored."

Harrigan gazed into the distance, as if he could see the Australians wait for hell to rain down.

"I'd use one of the Aerocobras," said Harrigan. "They got the cannon in the nose, and they're built like a tank."

"Built like a tank and flies like a tank. Don't do it."

Harrigan spoke. "It can't out-fly Zeroes, but I'm not fighting Zeroes. I'm going after those bombers. That cannon will blow the bastards apart."

The Chaplain said nothing. He topped off Harrigan's cup and refilled his own. If he drank enough, maybe the memory of the young pilot with coughed blood would go away.

"Why?" asked the Chaplain. "Why do it?"

"You know, when I was stateside, I was a no-good son-of-a-bitch. Got a girl pregnant. She and the baby live with her folks. She sent me a letter with the news, but I never wrote her back." Harrigan stood. "I got to do what's right."

"Getting killed won't fix anything."

Harrigan pointed to the distant firestorm. "There's a full moon tomorrow. Perfect for shooting down bombers. So. Would you bless the Aerocobra?"

Blessing an engine of killing: he did it all the time. The Chaplain was beyond considering the moral contradictions. "How about now?"

Harrigan patted him on the shoulder. "I knew you would. Proud you're in this man's army." He pulled a sweat-soiled envelope from his shirt pocket. "I need you to witness this. Make it official."

Pilots seemed to know when they weren't coming back. Maybe if the Chaplain had refused to take the envelopes, all those men would be alive. "Your will?" he asked.

"Sort of," said Harrigan. "I'm giving her my Death Benefit and war bonds for the baby. I figured you'd be the man to take care of it."

The Chaplain pointed into his tent. This time, he wasn't going to touch the letter. Maybe things would turn out differently. "Put it on my footlocker."

Exploding bombs flashed on the horizon, followed by the

rumble of man-made thunder. Death kept its appointment at Port Moresby.

*****

The moon hung large in the sky, its silver, pockmarked face throwing pale shadows. Men gathered on the airstrip, the red tips of their cigarettes mimicking the stars.

The whine of Harrigan's Aerocobra had faded into nothing. The jungle's night sounds were amplified by the silence. Men could hear their own breath as they waited and watched.

The trio of monstrous black flying things passed over the face of the moon, the rumble of their engines weighing in the air. A small streak—the size of a sparrow hawk—darted across the sky.

The click of a cigarette lighter filled the silence, followed by hushed whispers.

One of the black hulks dropped from the formation, gliding downward, leaving a trail of sparks.

"He got one!" A ragged cheer rippled across the airstrip.

A red string of beads appeared in the sky—tracers from the Aerocobra's cannon. "There!" shouted somebody. The men on the field expected another bomber to fall. They waited.

Another line of tracers. The second seaplane exploded into a fireball.

"He must be out of cannon ammo by now," said the

Chaplain. "God help him."

The wind changed, bringing the roar of the last bomber's engines. The airplane moved through the sky unhindered, like a storm cloud.

Time slowed. Nobody dared say a word. They could hear only one set of engines, and see the solitary black shape.

The last bomber dropped like a burning leaf, spinning earthward, out of sight.

The watchers scattered off the field. Drivers brought the fire truck and ambulance to life, and their headlights pierced the night.

Ditches along the airstrip exploded into a flaming path to guide Harrigan home.

Silence. No sound of the Aerocobra's engine, only the crackling of the fire. The stink of gasoline and burning greenery overcame the jungle air.

A sputtering engine split the quiet.

The Aerocobra materialized from the darkness, gliding onto the landing strip, and skidding in the dirt. It drifted to the left, rocked, turned, then to the right, but stayed true to its course.

Harrigan's plane came to a stop. The ambulance and fire truck rolled alongside.

One of the fire crew ripped off the engine cover, to be lost in oily smoke. He stumbled back, coughing, as his comrades tossed buckets of mud on the fire. Fire extinguishers were precious and saved for dire emergencies.

The Chaplain leaped from the ambulance onto the Aerocobra's wing and clambered to the cockpit. Harrigan was going to be there, alive and well.

The cockpit's glass was shattered, the instrument panel in pieces, the armor dented and dimpled. A shred of parachute silk fluttered in the breeze.

A torn parachute meant a dead pilot hanging in some distant tree. Thank God they don't have autumn here, he thought, or we'd be haunted by what the leaves conceal.

The rescue crew gathered at the cockpit, and like the Chaplain, looked but did not want to see.

Hollow inside, the Chaplain puzzled how an airplane—shot up, controls gone, engine burning—could land itself.

He should have refused Harrigan's envelope.

*****

The Chaplain slouched in the canvas chair outside his tent, hovering near exhaustion. In his lap, he held a canteen cup half filled with scotch.

The bombers never returned.

Harrigan's letter remained undisturbed on the footlocker. Pilots had come back before, a few times, carried in by friendly Aborigines.

Nobody came back after a week.

It would be seven days, tonight. He looked up from his cup.

Harrigan stood in the night, flight suit stained with dark splotches, his face dirty and pale. The Chaplain rubbed his eyes.

"Are you alive or am I asleep?" asked the Chaplain. The visitor said nothing.

The Chaplain delicately pushed the cork into the bottle. "Yeah. You're right. I should stop this. Save it for those who need it. Anyway, what good is a drunk Chaplain?"

Harrigan turned and walked towards the parked aircraft.

"I give up," called out the Chaplain. "I'll send your damned letter." His words hung in the air.

He stood and followed Harrigan for a few steps, knowing he wouldn't find him. He stopped. Looking skyward, he saw nothing but the black velvet of the tropical night, and its glittering chaos of a million stars.

A Killer of a Deal

The automobile gleamed in the twilight, the pearl color of a great white shark. Cliff ran his hand across the hood, with the same thrill and rush as if it was.

"It's a beast, alright," said the seller, an older man with a weathered face who wouldn't look Cliff in the eye. "Only two years old, less than twenty-thousand miles on it."

Cliff slid beneath the car. No welds where there shouldn't be, no re-bent metal…he saw no symptoms of concealed repairs. He ran his hand along the transmission seals and the bottom of the engine. His fingers came away dry with only faint streaks of street dirt.

"It was my wife's car," explained the seller. He stumbled over his words.

"Nothing…uh…happened to the, uh, car."

"The car wasn't in an accident?" asked Cliff. Maybe he had missed something when he looked underneath. "Can I take a picture of the car's VIN number so I can look it up?"

"Go ahead. It's a killer of a deal."

"It was your wife's car? What happened?" asked Cliff.

The seller looked down at his feet. "You marry them and

they're all sweet and once they got you hooked they reel you in and," He smacked his hands together like a gunshot. His eyes went wide for an instant. "I mean, uh, she just went out one day and didn't come back."

"Sorry," said Cliff. He'd be pleased if his wife walked away one day and didn't return. Then he reconsidered. No, he'd miss her. He reconsidered and realized, that reconsidering was why he was still married. It was nobody's fault. He made a bad choice. Or she did. Or they both did.

Cliff pushed away the uncomfortable thought by lifting the hood. The motor block filled the engine compartment. The fuse box, water pump, radiator, air intake, and hoses were all peripheral to the bored-out chunk of metal in the center. Everything under the hood was as clean and perfect as in the dealer's showroom.

"Only two years old and twenty thousand miles," repeated the seller.

This was too good to be true.

"I'd like to give it a test drive," said Cliff.

He reached down to touch the seat adjustment, but the steering wheel, gear shift, and the instruments were ergonomically perfect. Turning the key, the automobile rumbled softly, thousands of tiny gasoline explosions locked down by American steel. It ran through him like his own blood.

Cliff turned onto the highway. The motor purred, the velvet-smooth acceleration pressing them into their seats. He didn't really *drive* the car—it read his thoughts and desires, turned, accelerated, and braked, in a symbiotic relationship.

"Only ten thousand," said the seller. "Uh…it's a killer of a deal."

"Ten thousand?" Cliff echoed. The price was on the low side for a car in this condition.

"I'm willing to deal. "I don't want to bother with all the phone calls, people looking and not buying, that sort of thing."

On their return, Cliff negotiated an even lower price, emptied his checking account, and left with the car, a hand-written bill of sale, and the title.

For a moment he let himself savor the comfort of the seat, the feel and smell of an almost-new car. For sheer joy, he tromped on the accelerator and burned rubber. The car screamed out of the parking lot.

Cliff hurled himself through the front door of the garage.

"Jo-Ann? Jo-Ann? Want to see the new car?" he called.

He found her on the sofa, watching TV with her poodle, Snowflake, curled on her lap. She gently deposited the dog on the floor, then shot to her feet. "You did what?"

Cliff stumbled backward, and his excitement vaporized. "I bought a new car. The red one had been giving us trouble—"

"We only *talked* about a new car," Jo-Ann corrected. "We never *agreed*."

Cliff delicately phrased his response. "What matters is the red car isn't reliable."

"We *need* new drapes, kitchen cabinets, new wallpaper, and candle-sconces for the dining room." Jo-Ann pointed at herself.

"I *need* new clothes for work."

"I know. But if the red car stops running—"

"I have to look professional. You'll carpool with somebody." She wagged her finger at him. "Why didn't you ask first?"

Cliff took a deep, long, calming breath. "This never happens—perfect price, great shape, real, low mileage. And I thought we had agreed."

"We did not agree."

"But, I used my money," argued Cliff.

"Your money is our emergency money."

"You know I wouldn't do something like this unless I thought we agreed."

"Oh, God." She rolled her eyes. "Show me what you spent our money for."

Cliff held open the door to the garage. Jo-Ann halted on the last step, her voice incredulous. "It's white. You said you'd never own a white car."

"It's not white. It's a pearl. Sort of a silvery white."

She sighed, shaking her head. "Is it too late to get your money back?"

"It's a done deal," said Cliff. "There's no reason he'd give me back my check."

Jo-Ann approached the front of the car. "It doesn't leave much room in the garage." She shuffled her way around to the front. "It'll use too much gas."

Snowflake pushed open the screen door, bounded down the steps, and sat at her feet.

Jo-Ann gazed at the combined image of the headlights, bumper, hood, and air-intake. Her forehead furrowed. "It looks like it has eyes and a mouth," she said.

Snowflake sat at her feet and barked. Sharp, rapid, angry yaps, like it made when Cliff was slow with a treat.

She knelt beside the barking dog. "What's wrong, baby? No, I don't like it either."

Encouraged, Snowflake jumped up, resting its front paws on the bumper, its nose against the grill, the yapping reaching higher volume.

Jo-Ann bumped Cliff aside. "Don't you get it? There are the eyes, the mouth." She reached toward the grill. "See? Here's its—"

She shrieked. "It ate Snowflake!"

Cliff looked down at his feet. Snowflake was gone. "It's around here somewhere." He crouched down looking beneath the car, expecting to find the canine curse defecating precisely where Cliff would have to clean it up.

He heard Jo-Ann call behind him. "Snowflake! Baby! I'll get you out."

He heard her slap the hood with a thump. She stuck her hand inside the grill. "Cliff. My hand's stuck!"

Cliff ran back and peered into the grill to see only black. He ran his hand along hers. "Here, you must be caught on something."

"Get me out of this!" Her voice was high-pitched and angry.

"Let me open the hood," said Cliff. He flung himself across

the front, reached through the open window, and pulled the release.

She shrieked. Jo-Ann thumped against the bumper hanging by one hand.

His eyes went wide. Cliff pushed up the hood. Only engine, no hand. Not even Snowflake.

Jo-Ann yelped and disappeared up to her shoulder and hip. She flailed her free arm, and chopped the air into tiny pieces.

Cliff dropped to the floor and slid on his back, beneath the car. He couldn't see anything that didn't belong there.

"Do something!" Jo-Ann screamed.

He grabbed her arm and leg and pulled, gritting his teeth. "That hurts," said Jo-Ann. "Just get me out—"

She slipped from his grasp and disappeared through the grill of the car.

His heart stopped.

An engine. Radiator. Hoses. Spotlessly clean, an internal combustion maze.

He was in shock, that's it. In a few minutes the calm would wear off, and the horror explode inside him.

He walked around the machine as if he would find Jo-Ann hiding behind a fender, playing a bad joke on him. She wasn't.

He stumbled to the garage steps, sat, and stared at the car. Yes, it did look like eyes and a mouth. So did all the other cars of that model.

Cliff slammed down the hood.

Still in a daze, he took the keys and started the motor. It coughed. For a moment he smelled burnt dog hair, then only a new car smell. The engine purred.

Cliff cleared the shock from his mind.

He'd get rid of the car. He settled into the seat, and realized how it fit him perfectly. The engine rumbled in a soft low comforting way, and Jo-Ann wasn't yelling. He didn't miss her damned dog either.

He reconsidered.

He'll keep the car. It was a killer of a deal.

The Winter of Her Discontent

The staccato patter of little clawed feet wrenched Denise from sleep.

The squirrels scampered, played, and created a boisterous, rodentine racket. Their cheerful abandon angered her as much as the interrupted sleep.

She threw off the covers, stood on the bed, rocked and swayed in the worn mattress ocean, and banged against the ceiling with her fist.

Silence.

Denise collapsed, and beneath the blankets, anticipated the warmth of inherited home-made quilts.

Then, the squirrels danced a clattering quadrille over her head.

Denise hated them, but not as much as she hated her boss. She felt guilty about the squirrels; they were God's creatures. So was her boss, or so she was taught. Still, if he went somewhere and never came back, she wouldn't be upset.

She could do something about the squirrels, though, and do it now.

Denise dressed for work, then added a winter layer of floppy hat, thrift-store Navy pea coat, and sensible boots. She opened the kitchen cabinet for her keys. A heavy blur dropped past her face and brushed her nose. The object clunked in the sink, then with a whoosh, popped open.

That damned can of World Gourmet nuts. Her reward for saving the production from her boss's incompetence. The year before, everyone received a check in a holiday envelope, but last year they received brightly wrapped cans of mixed nuts. She was sure her boss got a nice, fat check. He went to Florida for a week.

Her anger smoldered. To open the can meant acceptance of the injustice. She couldn't do it.

Denise hefted the can and imagined bashing in her boss's head. Ashamed of her violent thoughts, she returned the can to the counter.

Get rid of the squirrels.

Outside, the world was grey, dawn's pause when early morning darkness struggled against sunrise. The air smelled of snow, heavy with moisture. From the porch, Denise could see the loose panel over the eaves. Dark, beady eyes looking back at her. Nutshells and acorn caps sifted down to hit her face. She imagined the creatures hidden in their cozy nook, the attic of her house paid for with a job from hell, as they laughed with squirrel giggles at her distress.

She glared with a look that would vaporize steel. "You and my boss are done for," a hollow threat for one of them.

Denise brought out a kitchen chair and broom. With the added height, she banged and prodded, slipped the broom handle under the eaves, and waved it around like The Grim Sweeper until her arm grew tired.

She let the broom fall to the porch. A moment later, little, obstinate eyes peered from the gloom.

"I warned you." Denise cursed and returned to the kitchen. She recovered the can of mixed nuts and yanked off the damaged lid. The edge sliced her hand in revenge, blood spraying the bright label. She grabbed a paper towel to staunch the bleeding and went to the bathroom to rattle through the medicine cabinet. She opened the box with her good hand, but splashed droplets of blood as she covered the wound with undersized band aids.

Like Joan of Arc, she returned to battle.

Outside, cold rain with ice pellet hearts started to fall. With her injured hand against the wall, Denise steadied herself and then climbed onto the kitchen chair. She shook a tiny pile of nuts on the cap of the pillar, sprinkled more at the base, and tossed a trail of jumbo gourmet cashews, brazil nuts, and pecans down the sidewalk.

The chair wobbled. She grabbed for the pillar, seeing herself crashing headfirst onto the concrete. She caught her breath, stepped down, and tried to become invisible in the corner. A pair of grey squirrels squeezed together on the pillar and picked up the bait in their paws. One of them pointed to the trail. Grey blurs zoomed past her onto the sidewalk.

"Got you!" Denise leaped onto the chair and reached overhead. The aluminum panel fought back, sharp edges nicked and sliced her fingers. After a push, a bend and a twist, the panel dropped into place. Women had not only mastered wild beasts, but sheet aluminum. She tapped it with her fist, satisfied with the solid fit.

Denise brought the chair inside and set the can of nuts on the counter. She clicked on the TV to hear a female reporter in a sleet-decorated beret tell everyone to stay home and not to drive. In the background lines of cars crept through the ice curtain. Denise had used her precious sick days being sick and expended her vacation to build her courage to return to work. She could be fired if she didn't show up. Worst of all, her boss would enjoy it.

She grabbed her purse and keys, locked the front door, and glanced up at her small victory, and smiled.

*****

Denise passed by spun-out and abandoned cars to arrive on location with teeth clenched and a death grip on the steering wheel.

Her boss started in before she was even out of the car. "We can't shoot!" he yelled. He paced, the ice beneath his feet too intimidated to do its job. "You!" he pointed at Denise. "We can't work! We only have exterior scenes! How could you do this to me?"

Denise took in a calming breath. "I told you to save the interiors for last."

"You failed to persuade me!" he shot back.

She looked to the crew for assurance. The actors studied their feet or pretended to be invisible. The union crew rolled their eyes, shrugged, and grinned. They got paid time and a half in bad weather. It was in their contract.

She chose her words. "Do you need me for anything? If we're not…"

"Aargh!" His mouth opened and closed, like a shark practicing its bite. "Go home!"

*****

An icy glaze covered the city. Bushes and trees became crystal sculptures and the grass, spun glass. Sleet froze on her windshield as fast as it hit, forcing Denise to set the defroster at its highest roar.

After the hell of every slip of the wheels, she took a wide, slow turn into her driveway. The car slid backward for a heartbeat, then stopped.

Something small, grey, and red lay on the porch.

She stepped onto the driveway and slipped. She fell against the car, clung to its icy side, then inched her way to the lawn. Frozen grass gave her sure footing and crunched with every step. The front door was only a few feet away.

The air was sucked from her lungs.

A dead squirrel lay on the cold concrete, its mangled coat matted crimson, mouth open to show chipped teeth smeared red. Denise glanced up at the aluminum panel. A crude hole had been chewed in the center and the edges glistened with blood. Little, bloody paw prints ran down the pillar, and ended at her feet.

She forced herself to breathe.

She had to get rid of the body. To leave it in the sleet felt wrong but to throw it in the trash was worse.

She felt obsidian eyes bore into her from the skeletons of leafless trees. In the garden, among her precious irises and gladiolas, she chopped through the ice to dig a squirrel-sized hole and lined it with an old towel. She slid the shovel under the squirrel, then returned to the garden and folded the towel in her best imitation of a burial shroud. The small grave lay dark against the blanket of ice crystals over the lawn.

Denise pulled her boots off in the kitchen, hung her coat and hat to dry, and walked into the bedroom to change clothes.

The empty nut can lay on her pillow.

Small claws clattered across the kitchen floor. She spun around in time to see a grey blur pass the doorway.

Her heart pounded loud enough she could hear it. She crept to the bedroom doorway. She heard a chittering taunt and saw a squirrel disappear around a corner.

She needed a weapon. The empty can was worthless. Her softball bat would be too heavy and the tennis racquet faster but too light. A skillet would be perfect.

Denise flung the can down the hallway as a diversion, then sprinted to the kitchen. She opened the cabinet and extracted her favorite pan, American made stainless steel. She tested the balance and a mote of confidence returned.

Her eyes strayed to the window. Squirrels gathered around the grave as fluffy-tailed mourners. She pulled shut the curtain.

The image of being slaughtered by angry squirrel mourners formed in her mind. She needed more than the skillet, something like the mini-pepper spray in her purse, left in the bedroom.

She sprinted to her room and grabbed her purse. Denise turned to see a squirrel now blocking her way out.

She popped the cap off the pepper spray and hefted the skillet in the most threatening manner she could muster. "Move!"

The squirrel's eyes widened. It cocked its head as if it

reconsidered its intentions, then turned tail, and scampered into the hall.

Denise put her back to the wall, and with the skillet in one hand, pulled out her phone. Her fingers brushed the screen as she searched for exterminators, then changed her mind. She had exterminated one squirrel by accident. That was enough. She found only one "Humane Pest Removal."

She pressed the icon, the phone buzzed, then answered.

"I have a squirrel emergency." She kept her voice steady. "They're in the house," she whispered.

"We can send a specialist tomorrow."

"How about now?"

"We can't work in this weather. Dangerous ice, you know."

She heard paws run down the hall. "How can I get rid of them? I had this can of nuts—"

"What kind of nuts? What brand?"

Denise visualized the label. "World Gourmet."

The voice lost its professional calm. "Throw them outside. Now! They're crack cocaine for squirrels."

She thought of the empty can. "It's a little late for that." She peeked out the bedroom window to see a row of squirrels perched on the sill, fluffy tail to fluffy tail. They looked back at her.

"What do I do until tomorrow?"

"Find a safe place, and whatever you do, get rid of those World Gourmet nuts."

Her phone's call-waiting beeped. Her boss. It was a touch of normalcy, rather than malevolent squirrels, so she answered.

"You have to wrap the Holiday gifts," her boss announced.

"Wrap? Gifts?" she screamed. "No bonus checks? Again?"

"It's wrong to expect a bonus. That's why it's called a bonus," he explained with all the certainty of somebody who just received one.

Denise tried to crush the phone in her hand like it was his neck. "You wrap them," she growled.

"You're the production assistant. I want you to do it."

"Want me to hand them out, too? With a little speech about teamwork?" She could taste sarcasm like blood on her tongue.

"That would be great," he said. "I have to get to the airport. I don't want to be late."

"Where are you going this time?" demanded Denise.

"Cancun."

Angry tears danced in the corners of her eyes. "I can't get out," she said. She started to say squirrels, realized the absurdity, and said, "Ice."

'No problem. I have four-wheel drive and high-performance radials."

Denise growled and paced, but there was nothing to kill.

The deep-throated diesel rumble of her boss's SUV invaded her house.

She watched the truck-wheeled monster come down the street and turn into her driveway. She cringed, expecting it to smash her car, but the bumpers barely touched. Her boss climbed out, leaned against the SUV for balance, and opened the back. He lifted a box with a loose roll of wrapping paper on top and took a step.

Wrapping paper bounced off the cans as he made a feeble attempt to grab it. The box crashed onto the sidewalk, and a pair of cans escaped, hit the ground, and popped open. Denise could hear him curse. He pushed the box onto the lawn, picked it up, and with slow, careful steps, put the box in front of her door. He went back to recover stray cans of World Gourmet mixed nuts.

She shoved open the front door. "Leave them!" she warned.

He looked at her as if she was demented. "No," he said, in his director's voice.

The squirrels raced him and won. He kicked one like a football. It disappeared with a squeal. He picked up the open can, triumphant, and reached for the second.

A squirrel leaped from the ice and sunk its teeth into his hand. "Let go!" The squirrel didn't. He smacked the squirrel into her mailbox with a metallic thump. He did it again and his curses drowned the racket. A wolf pack of squirrels ran across the lawn in a grey torrent.

He kicked and fought his way back to his SUV while squirrels hung onto him like grey Christmas ornaments. He wrenched open the door and rolled onto the front seat. The SUV rocked and swayed but the tinted windows hid the battle.

He shouldn't have kicked the squirrel like that, thought Denise. It wasn't their fault. It was the World Gourmet nuts.

She rehearsed her plan in her mind, then flung open the door, and began to rip the lids off cans like a chain reaction. Finished, she looked up.

The SUV stilled. The front windows whirred down, and blood-splattered squirrels poured out.

They stopped at the bottom step in a furry phalanx, little eyes dilated, noses twitching at the scent of World Gourmet nuts.

Denise reached down, picked up a can, and rolled it down the steps, to leave a trail of jumbo cashews, brazil nuts, and pecans.

The squirrels rocked side to side, wide-eyed, and fidgeted with their paws, but didn't move.

She rolled the cans one by one with a sense of satisfaction. There would be no demeaning holiday-wrapped cylinders this year. The icy ground was covered with mixed nuts. Still, the squirrels stood in silent ranks.

Denise didn't turn her back but opened the door and slipped inside. Her absence must have been the signal because a frenzied blizzard of squirrels raced for the nuts. She watched through the side window, puzzled.

They'd waited, waited until she was inside.

While the SUV was still like a coffin.

Denise pulled her phone from her pocket and debated calling 911.

Special Charter

Cliff struggled against the current of passengers and beeping golf carts rushing down the concourse. Passengers whose only reason to exist was to stumble along like sheep with baggage. Los Angeles traffic, the malevolent chaos of the airport, and checkpoint bottlenecks all contributed to his last-minute sprint.

As the gate numbers grew larger, the crowd grew thinner, and condensed to him alone. For once he wasn't dodging passengers frozen in mid-aisle or business travelers dragging their careers in their luggage. He jogged beneath burnt-out lights and passed gates with the imprints of extinct airline logos. The air smelled musty and dust motes danced in the sunlight.

Special Charters was the last.

He could see the jet outside the window, colors faded and scratched except for "Special Charters" freshly painted on the tail. Black stains streaked the wings and the engines were pockmarked and dented. The stench of jet fuel hung in the air.

At the counter, a crowd waited. An old man in a wheelchair, a beauty whose years had taken their toll, beside him. A young woman with limbs twisted and jerking. A man and woman older than Cliff's grandparents held hands.

"Your destination?" asked the woman at the counter of the couple who held hands. Her left arm trembled.

"The Lake of the Ozarks. Before the speedboats and party coves," he said. She smiled. "Confirmed."

The old man in the wheelchair was up next. He patted the woman's hand. "Auburn University. 1964." He reached out and patted her hand. "She was a tennis star."

Cliff watched the clock as the other passengers passed the counter. Boarding will take a long time with all these sick, old people, he thought.

Cliff pulled the paper copy of the boarding pass from his pocket. He couldn't find the site to make a copy on his phone. "This goes to St. Louis, right?"

The attendant smiled through terminal world-weariness. Too many friends lost their jobs, and too many airplanes were used as weapons. "Yes...." She turned her head and coughed in wrenching spasms. She took a cautious, shallow breath. When she spoke, her voice was strained and thin. "What time would you like to arrive?"

"It's a three-hour and half-hour flight?"

"It can be," she said.

"So, we'll arrive around eight o'clock tonight, right?"

"Earlier if you'd like."

"I guess because of tailwinds and weather and such?"

"Something like that."

"I'm all for early," said Cliff. For once flying weather would work for him, instead of creating interminable delays.

The door beside the counter was still open—he could make the flight. He thumped down the ramp, turned the bend, and saw the flight attendant in the open doorway.

The entire plane was first class. Cliff followed the aisle to his wide, soft seat and took a deep breath of recycled air.

A child, pale, baseball cap pulled down on a hairless head stood beside Cliff's seat. "I'm going to Disney World," whispered the child. "I have leukemia."

Cliff stumbled for the right words. "It's…good you're going to Disney World." The child pointed a thin finger to the bin over his head. "Could you please help me put my bag up there?"

Compared to the entire trip, a minor inconvenience. How could he refuse a little kid going to Disney World?

Cliff unbuckled and stood in the aisle, absently looking to the back. He saw a man his age, gray from chemo, and a young woman, her limbs contorted and a feeding tube in her neck, buckled in. Behind her was an old couple, the woman frail, a thin ghost in a print dress. Cliff looked away, to not be impolite.

One engine started, and its rumble turned into a healthy high-pitched whine. The second came to life, sputtered, belched black smoke, and hummed out-of-tune.

"May I have your attention, please?" asked the flight attendant. Cliff dropped into his seat.

The flight attendant lifted the stub of a seat belt and buckle. "Before we begin safety instructions…does everybody have a one-way ticket?"

A few feeble cheers filtered down the aisle. Cliff checked his ticket. One way.

She continued, "FAA regulations require you to fasten your seat belt and pull it snug." She snapped the buckle together to illustrate fastened bits of the belt attached to nothing. She grinned and tossed the prop over her shoulder. "Who cares?"

Cliff thought the same thing for years. In case of a crash, they'd all be dead; maybe seat belts made recovery of the bodies easier.

The airliner began to roll, the out-of-tune engine clanking. The attendant was caught off-balance, and after two attempts, grabbed an overhead compartment to keep herself upright. It didn't affect her announcement.

"We are now departing for Disney World, the Chicago World's Fair, Venice, Ireland, Palm Springs, St. Louis, and other destinations. Thank you for flying Special Charter."

Cliff pulled the ticket from his pocket—LAX to STL. He stood halfway in the aisle and waved to get her attention. "This flight goes to St. Louis, right?"

"Yes, it does."

Cliff collapsed in his seat. He didn't care where else it went as long as it took him home. The whole Hollywood screenwriting thing had only been a cash-induced illusion. He was getting out alive and with money left over.

The attendant began to cough again, as a chain of deep, wrenching spasms shook her body. She clung to the overhead compartment with one hand and pulled a handkerchief from her pocket to cover her mouth. She glanced at the contents of the handkerchief, betrayed nothing, and stuffed it back into her pocket.

The plane jolted, then vibrated to the runway. The attendant flipped down her jump seat, ignored her safety belt, and lit a cigarette.

Odd. Cliff glanced over his head to see the little image of a crossed-out cigarette, but he'd never been on a charter flight before, so maybe the rules were different.

The jet rolled to a stop with a squeal of brakes. In a few moments, the engine noise grew louder, the vibration dancing in the pit of Cliff's stomach, then the rush down the runway. Acceleration pressed him into his seat, the roar grew louder and reached the crescendo where he always felt he pushed the plane skyward.

Cliff's grip tightened. The airliner rose at a sharp angle, then leveled off.

An audible sigh, not necessarily of relief, filled the cabin. Cliff retrieved a two-inch-thick paperback from his carry-on bag.

A few pages in, the beverage cart rattled down the aisle. "Complimentary beverage, sir?"

"This flight goes to St. Louis, right?" asked Cliff. "I thought I heard other…." He pointed to the child beside him who was playing a video game. "This kid says she's going to Disney World."

"The flight continues to several destinations."

"I just didn't want to be on the wrong flight." Cliff relaxed. "Can you make a Manhattan?"

She peered into the shin-high compartment and rattled through a flock of miniature bottles. "Back when I started, we made fresh martinis, mimosas…. Sorry. No vermouth." She brought out several miniature bourbon bottles and laid them on the tray.

Cliff smiled at her efforts. "That'll do just fine."

He took two as shots and sipped the survivors while he read until the letters blurred.

The metallic hazy voice made an announcement. "We're currently approaching St. Louis International Airport." Cliff awoke, the taste of bourbon heavy on his tongue. The cabin was dark. He pressed the overhead light and a pale halo fell on the seat beside him. The child was asleep, crumpled against the window, the bald head peeking from the baseball cap.

Cliff half-stood and pressed the call button.

The darkness and bourbon obscured his vision. He didn't recognize the passengers. The woman with the feeding tube had been replaced by an athletic-looking girl in the same clothes. The old couple, now in their twenties, wore out-of-date clothes.

The plane tilted downward, and the pitch of the engines changed. "Sir, please take your seat," said the flight attendant in a smooth alto. She looked younger too.

"There's something wrong," said Cliff.

"Please take your seat." Her impatience added an edge to the words. He pointed to the sleeping child. "Is she going to Disney World?"

"Yes."

"But that's not the—"

The angle of the approach changed abruptly, threw him off-balance. He heard the familiar whir as the flaps extended for landing. "Take your seat." It was not a request.

Cliff feigned calm, collapsed into his space, and cinched the belt tight. He glanced at his watch. Something wasn't right. The watch said six fifty-five. Maybe they caught a tailwind. No, that wouldn't make up more than an hour. Probably he was just confused about crossing time zones.

The floor rumbled, and the landing gear dropped. New, aggressive vibrations shook the plane. The cabin shimmered, and for a moment, he was sitting in thin air.

Must be the four bourbons. Cliff closed his eyes, laid his head back, and waited.

The plane tilted left, then right. The approach seemed too steep. The rattling left engine complained more than ever. The air acquired a deathly chill. Cliff shivered.

The lights of the city rushed up. He had felt this before, the impression—they're just lights, and suddenly you see houses and cars. For a moment terror filled him. *Please God, no crash.*

The thump shook everything. Tires screeched. The plane bounced, brakes screamed, and engines roared in reverse.

The slowing plane felt like it taxied forever, then stopped with a jolt. Cliff watched the passenger stairs roll to the airplane's front exit.

The cockpit door slammed open. The pilot, who looked too old and too tired to still fly, glanced around with a scowl. He straightened and cleared his throat.

"Ladies and gentlemen, I apologize on behalf of Special Charters. There will be a slight delay. Someone has the wrong ticket."

The irritated murmur of healthy voices coursed down the

compartment. "This flight is one way. Everybody, get out your tickets!"

Cliff dug into his pocket and held up the paper printout of his paperless ticket. The pilot limped down the aisle, grabbed each piece of paper, held it to the light, and squinted. He came to Cliff, and stared into his eyes like he could read his soul.

He snatched away the ticket with surprising quickness. "Where'd you get this?"

"I bought it on eBay," said Cliff.

The pilot crumpled the paper and flung it at Cliff. It landed in the lap of the little girl, who woke up. "Are we at Disney World?" she asked.

The pilot growled. A cold, sinewy, old hand grabbed Cliff by the throat. "We can't continue the flight."

Cliff broke free of the old man's grasp. "What's wrong with you?" He rubbed his neck. "I'll just get off and the flight goes on."

"Can we try again?" asked a voice from the rear.

"I'll have to check with the tower. This has never happened before," answered the pilot. Cliff shoved past him and slipped into the aisle.

"That's not your ticket," growled the pilot.

Cliff didn't look back. He tripped over outthrust legs, and twisted away from grabby hands to reach the front hatch.

"Does this mean I don't see Disney World?" asked the little girl. "Everybody quiet!" ordered the pilot. "Let me think."

"What's going on?" demanded Cliff. "You aren't the same people this plane took off with."

"They are," said the pilot. "And you don't belong on this flight."

Passengers stood. A football player stepped into the aisle and came toward him. An athletic woman followed with a tennis racket in hand, held like a weapon. "Stop him."

Other passengers moved into the aisle, anger in their eyes.

"I'm supposed to go to Disney World," complained the little girl.

"Don't touch that hatch," the pilot ordered Cliff.

Cliff reached for the handle and searched for instructions. The football player slammed him against the cabin wall. Cliff clung to the handle. He yanked and pulled. He felt the pilot's hand the iron grip dig into his shoulder. Cliff pulled down. Left. Right.

The door fell open, and for a moment Cliff hung suspended. "Enjoy your trip," said the pilot.

Cliff crashed a dozen feet to the runway. No sound came out when he tried to scream. He blinked to clear the haze that filled his sight. He saw yellow flashing lights. Heard a siren.

Above him, the jet engines grew louder, into a deafening screech. He sensed the landing gear skim past.

The airliner's roar faded as the plane sped down the

runway and hurled itself into the sky.

A warm, calloused hand touched Cliff's neck, and felt his pulse. "Where the hell did he come from? This runway is locked."

Cliff saw worried faces. He pushed onto his elbow. Pain shot up his leg from his ankle. The air was heavy with humidity and a breeze carried the stink of jet exhaust. He was out of the airplane, and alive.

"Where am I?"

"St. Louis International."

"Hang on," said the other voice. "Security is on the way." Cliff squinted at his watch.

He had reached his destination. Early.

Disposal

Cliff passed through the sliding doors of the Home Everything and paused. The scent of sandalwood, cinnabar, and exotic spices teased his nostrils.

"You're picking up the garbage disposal." The voice evoked sex-goddess warrior queen, and cold-blooded business in the same breath.

He spun around.

Her features were…striking. Lips red as fresh blood, midnight colored hair. He gulped. There were no whites to her eyes, only the color of black obsidian.

She adjusted the name tag on her orange vest.

"Ashteroth," he read. The trivia part of his brain kicked into gear. "Ishtar. Astarte. Ancient Canaanite goddess." Cliff paused. "Goddess of sex and war."

She tapped him on the chest with a blood-red fingernail. "The one and only. I'm on a come-back tour."

"You're named after a goddess?"

"This way," Ashteroth said.

Aisle after aisle of power tools, lumber, tile, batteries, and nails passed by. She finally stopped beneath a ceiling sign the size of a truck — "Will Call".

Ashteroth slid a carton with odd lettering from the counter into Cliff's arms. "This is it," she said. "The disposal Jane asked for."

*****

Finished with the installation, Cliff flipped the switch. The disposal responded with a satisfying mechanical growl of whirring blades.

Job number one, install the disposal. Done.

Now, job number two, make supper.

He pulled a frozen brick of ground beef from the freezer and placed it in the sink to thaw.

The disposal ground furiously. The ground beef disappeared down the drain.

Cliff backed away. There was no way a whole plastic tray of ground beef could fit down a three-inch drain. He grabbed a cheap plastic flashlight from the drawer and peered down inside. No flecks of Styrofoam tray, no shreds of clear plastic wrapper. Not a trace.

Appliances don't turn themselves on. Not if wired right.

Cliff crawled under the sink and studied the garbage disposal. Three wires to connect—which he had done right—the sink drain and the hose to the plumbing.

Cliff took a can of beer from the fridge, and standing a safe distance from the unpredictable appliance, sipped and considered the concept of an appliance designed to dispose of unwanted items. He was still thinking when the front door opened.

Jane entered, glossy brochures in one hand, dragging her purse and briefcase. For an instant, surprise flickered across her face. "You're still here?"

"Yeah. I picked up the disposal. Put it in."

His wife stuffed the brochures into her purse. "Have you tried it? Does it work?"

"It works, alright. Watch." Cliff held the empty beer can over the sink.

The garbage disposal ground to life. He dropped the can and pulled away. The whirring blades went silent. The empty beer can rattled to a stop in the sink.

"What am I supposed to see?" asked Jane.

Cliff peered at the empty beer can lying across the drain.

"The thing sucked down a whole package of ground beef. Started by itself."

Jane gave him a look usually reserved for fibbing toddlers.

"Why didn't it take the can?" asked Cliff. "Maybe it's only carnivorous."

She laid her hand on his shoulder. "It's the stress. Losing your job…and we need two incomes."

"I can always cash in my life insurance. There's all that

money in my 401K."

"We agreed you wouldn't."

He sighed. "I really thought it sucked down a whole package of frozen meat."

"Cliff." Jane tried to sound comforting. "Sit down. Have another can of beer—"

"I got it!" He grabbed the handle of the refrigerator. "I bought two packages of ground meat. If one's gone, it really happened."

He swung open the door, and sticking his head inside, shuffled through unidentifiable wrapped, frozen things.

The frying pan smacked into his head, and he buckled into a heap.

He awoke wondering why he was draped over the kitchen counter. The disposal growled with enthusiasm as Jane dangled his hand over the drain.

Cliff pulled away. He lost his balance and slammed Jane into the counter. Stumbling, she thrashed out her arms for support and reached into the sink.

Jane screamed—a piercing, truncated wail. The disposal sucked her arm to the shoulder. Her mouth moved, but only choking sounds came out. In a heartbeat only a leg stuck upright in the drain. The foot wriggled in desperate protest, then spun out of sight. For an unpleasant moment, the disposal crunched and ground.

Then it switched off.

Cliff peeked over the countertop. The sink gleamed as clean as when he had scrubbed it.

The doorbell chimed.

Panic exploded inside him. The police. They found out— Ridiculous. Nobody knew. Answer the door like nothing happened.

Ashteroth stood on the front porch.

"Hmmm," she said, her eyes narrowing.

"That garbage disposal ate my wife!"

From beneath raven-wing eyebrows, Ashteroth attacked him with a knowing smile. "Nobody will believe you."

Slipping by, she opened the cabinet and with a flick of the wrist removed the carnivorous appliance.

"Things always have a way of working out," she said.

"But my wife—Jane—she's dead!"

"Not necessarily." Brushing back her ebony hair, she gave the unit several shakes. Maybe it was Cliff's imagination, but he could hear voices from inside. Lots of voices, screaming for help.

"There are people in there?" he asked.

"Only males," she said. "With the exception of Jane."

"Why only men?"

"Because I'm female. And I didn't say, men. I said, males. There's a difference." She gave the disposal another shake.

"What about Jane? Can I get her back?" he asked.

"She just tried to dispose of you."

The bump on Cliff's head throbbed.

"Yeah…but…" Why want her back? He remembered he felt smaller and smaller after he lost the job. Jane pushed to take over the credit cards.

Ashteroth was right.

Anger converted itself into courage. "How much did Jane pay for that thing?" he asked.

Ashtoreth named a figure. "Rented, not purchased."

Something dark and disappointing grew in him. "She used my severance money. I can't believe Jane…what do I tell everybody?"

"Not my problem. You're the one who rearranged fate."

He didn't see her leave or hear the door close.

On the kitchen table lay one of Jane's brochures, 'Romance Cruises.' He dumped out her purse, sorted through tissues, a wallet with credit cards he didn't recognize, lipstick, keys, two pens, and a cruise ticket for one passenger.

He had no idea Jane was unhappy. He'd no idea she could be so evil, so duplicitous. Maybe she didn't tell him, or she told him and he didn't listen, but she always complained about something…

What if there were more like him in the garbage disposal? Shoved down the drain by wives who planned cruises…imprisoned, hot and cold garbage sludge poured over their heads…he had to do something.

Days later, in an orange Home Everything vest slipped off the hook in the restroom, Cliff smuggled a garbage disposal in a carton with odd lettering into his car. He ripped off the vest and drove home, glancing into the rear-view mirror every two minutes.

He laid the unit on the kitchen table, loosened the screws, and opened the casing. Of course, there was nothing inside but wire and gears and blades.

For some reason he had expected to find scores of victims grateful for liberation.

He studied the wiring. As is, the disposal sucked things in. What if he reversed the wires?

He finished the work and installed the unit into the sink. Cliff flipped the switch.

The appliance ground and growled. First Jane's foot, then her leg, then all of her was spit out. She landed with a soggy thump on the floor. Sitting up, she blinked, looked at Cliff in shock, and then at the sink.

He expected some sign of gratitude. Instead, Jane threw herself at him, hands around his throat.

The brick of ground beef escaped next and bounced off the ceiling. Jane glanced up at the flying beef, and Cliff was able to pry her hands from his neck.

A man Cliff's age with lipstick on his cheek flew out of the sink. Next, an unshaven young man in a dirty T-shirt was flung out, followed by a lawyer, a used car salesman, another lawyer, a cable repairman, a tattooed gangbanger in an over-sized basketball jersey and a bullet hole through his head, and, last, a third lawyer.

The kitchen was clogged with people who all asked versions of the same question in loud, excited voices.

"I don't know!" shouted Cliff.

"As the owner of this garbage disposal, you're responsible," announced one of the lawyers.

The man with the lipstick smear scratched his head. "How'd she find out about me and her sister?"

"All of you," shouted Cliff, "Get out of my house!"

"Our house," corrected Jane.

Cliff opened the front door and shoved the ungrateful rescued—the ones that were alive—out, one by one.

Jane looked at him with emotion, but not affection. "It wasn't supposed to happen this way."

"You tried to kill me!"

"I didn't want to kill you. Just get rid of you."

Cliff grabbed the Romance Cruise brochures. "So you could go on a cruise?

"Ashteroth said you wouldn't be hurt."

"No! Just stuck in a garbage disposal for eternity!"

Jane shook her finger like she was brandishing a knife. "I should never have settled for you. I deserve better. I want to go on cruise like everybody else. See the world."

Cliff slammed open the kitchen cabinet and tore away at the garbage disposal's connections.

Yanking out Ashteroth's unit, he dropped it with a crash onto the kitchen counter.

"What are you doing?" demanded Jane.

"Fixing this god-damned thing. Or goddess-damned thing."

"Fix it?"

Cliff pointed to the two dead men on the floor. "We got to get rid of them."

He opened the unit's casing. Ripping the wires from their connections, he reversed them to the original pattern.

Cliff hefted the garbage disposal. It was a lot lighter than before.

"You going to hit me with a frying pan again?"

She mimicked his voice. "No. I'm not going to hit you with a frying pan."

On his back, he crawled beneath the sink. Cliff didn't take his eyes off Jane as he jammed the unit in place. He tightened the connections. Last, the wires.

For one instant, he had to look at the plumbing joint.

The food processor came down at his head. It nicked his

ear and crashed to the floor. Jane scrambled for a frying pan hung over the sink. Flat on his back, all Cliff could do was kick at her legs.

She fell forward, onto the sink.

The garbage disposal awoke, grinding and growling.

Jane flailed her arms to regain her balance, and…it happened again.

This time, Cliff didn't watch the struggle as she spun out of sight. He moved quickly, lifted the dead men, and pushed the bodies into the sink. He ignored the grind and crunch of the blades. The gangbanger with the bullet hole was next, and last.

Cliff caught his breath. The garbage disposal turned itself off. He glanced into the sink.

Shiny stainless steel clean.

He grabbed his tools, took out the unit, and shoved it back into the carton.

The doorbell rang and Ashteroth let herself in.

Cliff had twice escaped a murderous wife. His adrenaline was pumping and his confidence was high. He pointed to the garbage disposal. "You made a deal with Jane that this thing would dispose of me, right?"

Ashteroth glared darkly.

Not being turned into a pillar of salt or pummeled with brimstone made Cliff braver. "Well, I'm not disposed. Which means you can't take it back yet. Goddesses have to keep their deals, or they look bad, right?"

Black fire shimmered in her eyes, but Ashteroth said nothing.

"I just need it for a couple of weeks." Cliff pulled a sports bag from the closet and dropped the garbage disposal inside it. "Jane wanted to see the world and go on a cruise." He picked up the solitary ticket and zipped shut the bag.

"At least she'll get half of what she wanted," he said.

Ashteroth did not smile.

Five Stars

"Loser!"

Cliff drained the beer can, focusing his eyes on the source of the insult. A winged monkey — bristly grey fur, tail curled behind, wings folded — perched on the railing of his apartment balcony. Its beady eyes followed as he delicately stacked the empty can on the growing tower. Cliff popped open another, and the creature responded with a wide, toothy grin.

Taking a long slurp, he lowered the beer to see a second monkey land beside the other. This one wore a gas mask.

"This the right address?" it inquired.

The first consulted its phone. It nodded confidently.

"Why da gas mask?" it asked.

"'Cause he's a STINKIN' loser!"

The simians rocked back and forth in hysterical laughter.

Cliff struggled to sit upright in the plastic lawn chair. He was in no mood for verbal abuse. He had no girlfriend, no job, and no prospects of either. He was reduced to doing odd jobs to supplement his unemployment checks.

"Flying monkeys," he commented with the calm objectivity provided by four beers.

"Simia volaticus," corrected the know-it-all in the gas mask.

Cliff responded by taking another drink, cautiously peering over the can's rim.

A third monkey fluttered down to join his compatriots.

It lifted the sunglasses precariously balanced on it snub nose. "Knock knock," it said.

"Knock knock who?" came the predictable chorus.

"Loo."

"Loo who?"

"Loo-ser!"

The monkeys laughed riotously, wiping tears from their little, beady eyes.

"Shove off," growled Cliff. He flung the can at the intruder wearing the gas mask. It easily dodged the aluminum missile, cocking an ear toward the ground in response to the hollow clank.

"He 'beer'-ly missed me!" it announced.

The monkeys howled in laughter, holding onto each other to keep from falling off the railing.

Cliff staggered up from his chair. "Fuck you." He recovered the surviving beers and yanked open the porch door.

From nowhere, a man-sized canvas bag dropped over him. He struggled—punching, twisting, kicking, only to feel restraining ropes tighten.

He paused to think through his predicament. Flying monkeys had tied him in a bag. Houdini had escaped from such restraints—but then, he wasn't Houdini.

Apparently, his captors were more interested in shock and awe than results. After a nail-pulling effort, he had untied the knots from inside and pulled the bag from over his head.

Cliff whipped open the door and stumbled into his apartment. He groaned.

His meager furniture was overturned. Bookshelves were emptied, their contents scattered over the floor. Stale cigar smoke hung in the air, spiced with the odor of burnt cooking. From the kitchen came the clatter of plates, pots, and raucous drunken merriment.

Stepping over empty beer cans, books, and frozen food wrappers, Cliff tip-toed to the kitchen door and eavesdropped.

A bottle clanked onto the counter. "Last—(hiccup)-brown booze," rasped a simian voice. The distinctive pop of an opening beer can followed. "Let's burn something."

Cliff was cold sober now, and things would be different this time. He carefully planned his attack, then threw himself into the kitchen.

The floor was smeared with catsup, mustard, and things he didn't want to identify. Flying monkeys were scattered on the counter, in the dining set chairs, and passed out on top of the refrigerator.

Cliff ripped open a cabinet door and pulled out a heavy pitcher. He wielded it like Samson swinging the jawbone of the ass. Scattering his enemies, he slammed one creature in its furry chest. The simia volaticus bounced across the table, smacked into the wall, and flopped to the floor.

"Get out of here!"

Swinging again, he slapped a flying monkey against a cabinet. It screeched in pain, but clung tightly to the pitcher, wrapping its tail around Cliff's hand. Another tackled his leg, and he pounded it with his combined monkey-pitcher cudgel. The creature on the refrigerator popped awake and flung itself at Cliff. He batted the monkey out of the air with self-amazing dexterity. Astonished by his hand-to-monkey combat skill, he flailed away with the monkey-clad pitcher—bashing a swath through snapping jaws, clutching hands, and grasping tails.

A second monkey clambered onto the pitcher, rendering the weapon useless. Prying it off, Cliff yanked open the oven door and flung the original monkey-pitcher combination inside. Then, ripping the electric can opener from the outlet, he swung it by the cord, mowing down his chattering enemies. The oven door squeaked open, and he slammed it shut with his backside.

His winged tormentors rallied into a monkey-phalanx, hooting and encouraging each other for a counterattack.

Cliff pulled open the kitchen tool drawer, grabbing the hammer. Adrenaline rushed through him, the fire of combat burning in his eyes.

"Come on you Wizard of Oz rejects," he challenged. "Come and get me."

"Man, you could hurt somebody," whined one.

"Yeah, it's like this is your stuff…" added another like he was speaking from a pulpit.

"It's my apartment!"

"Au contraire, you merely rent," countered the monkey-preacher.

Cliff felt fists desperately pounding the oven glass. He pressed his full weight against it.

His first victim had regained consciousness, staggered up on all fours, and delicately examined its tail. Satisfied, the monkey shook its wings and stretched to its full two-foot height. Pointing a murderous finger, the creature growled in a low-voiced mock Austrian accent. "I'll be back."

The Dorothy nemesis crew fled the kitchen. Cliff heard the porch door slide open, then a barrage of parting insults, followed by flapping wings.

"Let me out of here." The voice from the oven wasn't that of a monkey.

Cliff crouched, and peered through the oven's little glass window. He saw a female human face graced with ocean-blue eyes and perfect eyebrows. A torrent of blonde hair covered her shoulders.

Hefting the electric can opener as a precaution, he pulled open the oven door about an inch and peeked inside.

"Please let me out." Her voice progressed from plaintive to demanding.

Cliff complied.

She poked out her head, retreated, slipped out a slim arm and shoulder, then huddled inside. "Uh, Could you get me something to wear?"

Cliff bounded from the kitchen, leaped over catsup and mustard puddles, skipped over living room rubble and debris. He hesitated at the bedroom—he could just give her a towel…no, it might be too small. Going to the closet, he examined his limited wardrobe. Something long enough…something easy to pull on… Flipping through hangers, he found a grey button-down dress shirt and ran back to the kitchen.

She had advanced onto the door but had managed to maintain some degree of physical modesty. He could still glimpse a lithesome thigh, a finely toned shoulder, the soft curve of a breast…

Cliff offered the shirt. "I think it's big enough."

She nodded, and clutched the shirt to her chest. "You

know, you can leave now."

Stepping over the condiment puddles, he paced back outside the kitchen and wished he had a beer.

After a few moments, in a less than confident voice, she called him back.

She'd rolled up the sleeves. The front and back shirttails barely covered the subject.

"Where am I?" she asked, her voice a mix of emotions.

"In my apartment." Cliff struggled to prevent his eyes from wandering over the shortcomings of the impromptu clothing. He tried to compensate by offering more information. "This is St. Louis. It's March thirty, two-thousand twenty-three."

Her eyes went wide. "Two thousand twenty-three?" she squeaked. Her shoulders shook and an explosion of sobs poured out and caused tears to streak down her cheeks. "A year," she gasped. She swiped at the tears with her sleeve without much result.

Cliff fidgeted, not sure how to comfort a woman, formerly a winged monkey. In a moment of inspiration, he slipped past her to recover the last handful of unburnt paper towels.

Sniffling, she accepted his offering. "You saved me," she said, her voice hushed.

She stepped nearer, blue eyes locked onto his. "It was horrible. They made me one of them. All the time, I knew…" The tears poured again. "You saved me!" Arms open, she crushed herself to Cliff. She molded her body to his and kissed him fiercely. In that instant, impressions flooded him—flawless skin, tongue seeking his, her hips against his groin....

Only a tiny part of his mind heard the fleshy 'pop'. Something sinuous caressed his thigh. Bristly grey fur exploded through her cheeks. Her teeth became sharp needles. Cliff jerked his head away, watched her eyes change to dark buttons, the nose flattened, widened, and her whole form shrunk to a simian likeness. He tried to push away, but the sinewy monkey arms clung around his neck. With a desperate effort, he broke the creature's grip.

It fell to the floor, still bundled in the shirt. Small furry hands reached from inside and unbuttoned their way out. Cliff stared wide-eyed. The monkey shook out its wings and grinned.

"Gotcha!" Hooting in triumph, it bounced off the apartment walls. Paused for a moment, the creature blew him a kiss, then spread its wings and leaped into the air.

Cliff watched it shrink to a distant speck, the howling guffaws fading. He turned in a slow circle, and surveyed the wreckage—empty liquor bottles, cigar ash, broken plates, books flung in abandon, scraps of food painted on the walls.

"Why me?" Cliff screamed.

He pounded the floor with his fists. He shouted complete paragraphs of obscenities, strung together new and unheard of epithets.

His phone's ringtone caught his attention. Out of pure

instinct, he answered the call.

"Mr. Browning, I represent Flying Monkey Quality Assurance. May I ask a few questions about the quality of our harassment—"

Cliff tried to crush the phone in his hand. "The name is Brown! There's no Browning here!"

The monkey voice at the other end hesitated. "This address isn't six-one-oh-five Afton Way?"

Six-one-oh-five was his neighbor. His BMW parked-in-two-spaces, loud-parties, screaming-girlfriend neighbor.

"This is six-one-oh-six," he roared into the speaker. "Brown! The name is Cliff Brown!"

"Are you sure?" it responded, minus its maniacal confidence.

"I know my name! This is Cliff Brown!"

There was a long silence, followed by panicked voices in hurried discussion.

"Thank you for your five-star ratings," said a maniacal simian voice. The line went dead.

Cliff punched redial. No such number.

MeggaPizza

The doorbell rang.

For a moment, Cliff imagined a friendly brunette outside his door, full of energy and personality, with a glittering smile. Anything was possible.

He opened the door.

A young man with a Black Death Jam T-shirt and MeggaPizza baseball cap held three large pizza boxes.

"I didn't order anything," said Cliff.

The boxes were balanced on one arm, the teenager studied the ticket stuck to the top.

"You Cliff Brown? One sausage, one pepperoni, one pineapple. Debit card, it says."

"I don't have a debit card."

The young man read off a cell phone number.

"That's my phone, but I didn't order anything," said Cliff.

"They're paid for."

What the hell, spend the money while he had it. Cliff dug into his pocket and offered a five-dollar tip.

He shut the door and stacked the boxes on the kitchen counter. The aromas of pizza sauce, sausage, and spices filled the room.

Cliff shrugged and opened one. Pineapple baked into the sauce and cheese formed the word ANSWER.

He squeezed his eyes shut and looked again. ANSWER.

He flipped open the next box. The sausage formed four letters. D-O-N-T.

Curiosity's momentum made him rip open the next box without thinking.

The pepperoni read PHONE.

He took a step back and stared.

It couldn't be a genuine message—there were better ways to communicate. You could maybe believe words on a birthday, farewell, and anniversary cake. On free pizzas? No.

It was free pizza. Maybe an omen of good things to come. He pulled out a slice and bit off the tip. He savored the tomato sauce, the cheese, and the hint of spice.

Good, but still a little too hot.

His cell phone buzzed. Cliff twisted the phone around with his free hand and read the caller ID. MeggaPizza. Calling to get their pizzas back? To charge him when he didn't order? He took the call. "Hello?"

A deafening sucking sound roared in his ear.

The three-word warning flashed through his mind too late. A vacuum pulled him headfirst. He felt himself shred into atomic particles and rode the cell phone microwaves on a stomach-churning roller coaster.

His eyes popped open.

He stood in a small, windowless, one-room apartment. Too much stuffed into the space—a bed, a nightstand with a photograph, a wall-sized TV. The smallest bathroom in the world and a rack of blue and yellow restaurant uniforms.

Still dizzy, he collapsed on the bed. The photograph was in his line of sight.

A woman. Dark hair, eyes that glimmered with intelligence, energy, personality, and a lot of other good things he couldn't name. She wore a blue and yellow fast-food uniform.

"Cliff Brown! Time to wake up!"

Cliff jumped up and spun in the direction of the sound. The TV showed a female cheerleader in a MeggaPizza sweater bouncing with manic enthusiasm. She backflipped out of the picture, and the company logo filled the screen.

Cliff remembered the phone call. He fumbled in his pocket for his phone and pressed re-dial.

One ring. He was certain he'd hear the sucking sound again, feel himself shredded, and end up where he started.

"MeggaPizza." The voice came from outside the door.

He dialed 911. No signal. He pushed the speed dial for his friend Whitney. No signal. He tried Mom. No signal.

"Customers!" blared the TV. The cheerleader did a summersault, landed and pointed her finger at him. "Cliff Brown! You have customers!"

Customers? Somebody else's, not his.

He marched to the door.

Cliff froze in the mirror. He wore a blue and yellow uniform, with the MEGGAPIZZA stitched across his chest. He gritted his teeth and reversed the backward reflection of the name tag. Cliff Brown.

What was he doing in this uniform?

He grabbed the door handle and pulled.

The smell of cooking pizza washed over him. Men and women in blue and yellow scurried around the pizza kitchen, shouted orders, answered phones, and carried boxes to the front. Customers in a dozen different fast-food uniforms—Chicken Supreme, Burger Barn, Indian Express—he didn't know how he knew the names—crowded the counter to pick up their orders.

She was there, the woman from the photograph. The woman he imagined outside his apartment door.

She turned and gave him a smile with a little wave. For that instant the noise ceased, swept away by her eyes and smile.

He was frozen in place when she hugged him. He felt her press every part of herself to him, unrestrained.

"No hug back?" she asked.

Cliff squeezed back. He wasn't sure why, but it felt natural.

"See you next shift." She handed him an oversized ring of keys.

Cliff looked at the keys, tried to think what to do, and failed.

"Cliff, are you OK?" she asked. "You don't look right."

"I'm not myself," he answered.

"See you third shift." She gave him the smile from the photograph and walked toward the rear of the restaurant. He turned to watch as she pulled off her MeggaPizza cap, and her dark hair cascaded. She opened a door in the back wall, and Cliff caught sight of a room much like his.

He should have looked at her nametag.

He called after her. "Excuse me, I—"

A dozen close-spaced doors bounced open at the back of the restaurant, spewing out people in blue and yellow uniforms. Mimicking the cheerleader's attitude, they exchanged places with the other employees—stood precisely at the same spot, picked up the same pizza boxes, fingers over the same touchscreens.

Cliff gulped. The mall's food court sprawled into the distance. He traced the restaurant signs—Mexican, burgers, Greek, Indian, more burgers, Chinese, Chicken Five Ways, burgers again—until the signs were too far away to read.

"Uh, like, uh, you're in my way."

Cliff turned to see a young man with pimply skin, his greasy hair tucked under a MeggaPizza cap. His name tag said Jerry. Beside him, a tomato sauce-splattered conveyor belt spewed out pizzas.

"Have you ever seen the toppings make words?" Cliff asked.

Jerry whipped an empty box from a stack and caught a veggie pizza as it dropped off the conveyor belt. "No way. Every pizza has the same consistent quality."

The cheerleader's voice boomed through the food court, and bounced off the walls.

"Cliff Brown! You have won the Promotion Lottery!"

"What's the Promotion Lottery?" asked Cliff.

Jerry's mouth dropped. "It's what every associate dreams of! Their name being picket out of the blue and yellow bucket—"

A pizza slid off the conveyor belt, and splat on the floor in a shrapnel of sausage and pepperoni.

"I'm not gonna pay for that,' said Jerry.

A torrent of blue and yellow balloons dropped from the ceiling, landed on employees, the kitchen floor, and unboxed pizzas. Stray balloons settled on the conveyor belt, and popped as they were caught in the rollers.

A man and woman in blue and yellow business suits bounded over the front counter. "We're the Promotion Team!" they shouted.

The woman pushed in front of her partner. "Cliff Brown! Your number was picked at random from hundreds of entries! You're on your way to a fabulous new Promotion!"

Her associate took Cliff's arm. He shook himself free. "I'm not the Cliff Brown you're looking for. I don't belong here."

The woman who hugged him burst from her door in the back, arms outstretched. She slammed into Cliff at a run and pulled him close. He felt her tears as she nestled her head between his neck and shoulder.

"You've been promoted," she sobbed. "I'll never see you again."

"I don't understand."

"But, of course, you have to go." She sniffed and wiped her eyes. "It's been a wonderful six months, Cliff." She hugged him again and with a whisper, "It has to be, but I'll miss you."

A blizzard of blue and yellow confetti dropped. Cliff was blinded and she slipped from his grasp. "What's your name?" he called. He pushed his way through the confetti storm. "Where are you?"

"Meggapizza! MeggaPizza! MeggaPizza!" poured out of loudspeakers.

The Promotion Team grabbed Cliff and propelled him backward.

Cliff broke away. "Keep your hands off me."

An electric shock ran through him and filled his vision with fireballs. He woke to find the Promotion Team had stuffed him into a yellow and blue golf cart. The vehicle lurched into gear and whirred away.

He tried to form words of protest, but only garbled noise came out.

The woman pointed a stun-gun at him, its tip crackling with blue electricity. She grinned like a tigress. "I like using this."

Her associate drove and looked over his shoulder. "Cliff, keep things in perspective. This is your promotion. Your career is what counts."

The numbness started to wear off. Cliff struggled to turn his head. He sounded like he had spent a day in a dentist's chair. "I'm not the Cliff you want. I don't belong here."

"How hard did you zap him?" asked the driver.

She responded with an artificial smile. "His name is Cliff Brown and he just won the Promotion Lottery."

The electric shock still buzzed through Cliff's brain, but he forced out the words. "I didn't enter a lottery."

The woman twisted Cliff's head toward her and held the stun gun to his nose. "Work with me or you'll end up in the Unemployment Draft."

The golf cart slowed with a screech of brakes and stopped at the elevator.

The doors whooshed open and a symphonic arrangement of Eighties rock music poured out. The Promotion Team pulled Cliff to his feet and shoved him inside.

The front door swished shut, the elevator climbed, and its back door slid open.

Row after row of office cubicles spread out as far as he could see.

A grey-haired woman popped around the corner and grabbed Cliff's hand.

He pulled away.

"C'mon," she pleaded. "I won the Retirement Lottery and can't leave until you're trained."

"You have the wrong person."

"No, I don't. You got promoted."

"By lottery?" asked Cliff.

"It's the only fair way."

She reached for his hand again but Cliff dodged her.

"It only takes a minute. Please?" she whined. "You just click on the 'OK' button."

The electric buzz from the stun gun lingered, but he couldn't resist the question.

"What am I okaying?" he slurred.

"Nobody knows. Who cares?" Her eyes grew hard and her grip tightened. "I get to retire."

Cliff ran.

Row after row of cubicles passed in a blur as he jogged down the hall, then slowed to a stop. He stood in a rat's maze of workstations. He should have spent less energy being angry, and more paying attention to where he was going.

The lights in the office blinked.

"Quitting time!" announced a chorus of voices.

Cubicles spewed a blue and yellow employee horde that pushed its way through the mobs. Cliff clung to a vacant cubicle and resisted the current.

The rush of bodies thinned. Now was the time to escape. The office had to have an outside wall, and an outside wall would have a door.

Cliff passed legions of cubicles, a giant room labeled Happy Hour, with cigarette smoke, loud music, and incoherent conversations pouring from its entrance.

A beige, featureless wall loomed before him. The door was only a few cubicles away. At eye level, in small blue and yellow letters were the words THIS IS NOT AN EXIT. Cliff pushed the door open. No alarm, no flashing lights, no sirens.

The door led to a stairway. He stopped to think through his next step. The door might lock behind him and trap him in the stairwell. He wedged his MeggaPizza cap into the lock.

At the bottom of the stairs was another door, the same beige color, with the same warning. Bits of dirt and trash littered the floor with scraps of food wrappers and crushed plastic straws.

He shoved the door open.

Cliff blinked in the golden glare of the setting sun. The air was cool, not uncomfortable, but crisp enough to let him know he was alive. In front of him sprawled a parking lot, its lines faded, and an occasional dumpster tipped onto its side.

"That's my door," said a woman's voice.

She wore remnants of assorted fast-food uniforms. Her red hair was sprinkled with grey, and she looked clean, scrubbed.

"I didn't know it was your door."

She looked him up and down. "You look like a newbie. You don't know any different." The woman held out her hand. "I'm Athena."

He shook hands. "I'm Cliff." He looked down at his uniform. "Not this Cliff."

"Your uniform says 'Cliff'."

"That's the problem. I don't belong here. I just came out of…" he gestured behind.

"We all did," she said.

"We? You escaped?"

"Anything is better than living in that beige climate controlled fast-food hell," she answered.

"Where do you live?"

She pointed toward one of the dumpsters on its side. "You just empty one out and get help tipping it over."

"Don't they try to get you back?"

She walked to a nearby dumpster shoved against a steel garage door. "They never have before. They just push out another one. Must have an infinite supply." She lifted the lid. "Since you're the newbie, you have to get supper. In you go."

With the mention of supper, he realized he hadn't eaten since that nibble of pizza in his apartment. He tried to compute how long ago and gave up when his stomach growled.

Cliff peeked inside the dumpster. He smelled fast food. Fresh. Not the usual sour stink of garbage. He pulled himself to the edge, then swung himself inside.

He stood on pizza boxes, fried chicken buckets, and burger bags. He bent to select a pizza box, half expecting it to have a message. The pepperoni was scattered across the cheese at random.

"This doesn't look like garbage. It all looks good. Why throw away good food?" he asked.

"That's the way it is," she answered. "Find me a pizza."

Pizza and its ramifications made his stomach twist, so he selected a bag of tacos for himself.

"Want to join me for dinner?" she asked. Athena pointed to a dumpster, next to a small mound of dirt with a few struggling daisies.

At her dumpster, Athena pulled out stools and a short table made of duct taped pizza boxes.

Cliff craned his head back and watched grey dusk creep across the deep blue sky. He could smell distant greenery and the fresh air of unconfined spaces. Images of his former life came to mind, followed by the tearful face of the girl who hugged him goodbye in Meggapizza.

"How did you escape?" Cliff asked.

"Just walked out," she said. "Had to leave or go crazy." Athena opened her pizza and studied the sausage scattered over the cheese. "Did you ever imagine the toppings made patterns?"

Cliff put down his burger. "That's how I got here. Some kid shows up with three pizzas and the toppings made the words. Don't answer the phone, they said." He dug into his pocket and pulled out his cell phone. "I answered the phone and got sucked through it into MeggaPizza."

He dialed Whitney's number. No signal. He slid it into his pocket.

Athena stopped eating and stared at him. "Sucked into this place by cell phone? That's pretty bizarre."

"Honest to God, that's what happened."

Athena turned her pizza around to examine the sausage from different angles. "Hmmm. No words."

She selected another slice. "You can join us," she said. "Life is good. Fresh air, nice weather, free food. You're a free person out here."

"Where are we?" he asked.

"Feels like California? Some people walked out and never came back. There's a dumpster of books from a store. I'm working my way through them."

Cliff rolled her words over in his mind. He sat back and

watched the darkness creep across the sky. He could make out hints of stars.

"There's this girl back at MeggaPizza," he said. "There's something about her. I need to see her again." He shrugged and bit into his burger. "Chemistry, I guess."

"You can go back in," said Athena. "We do it all the time." She waved around. "You don't see any bathrooms out here, do you? We use the executive baths on the third floor. Gold plated faucets, crystal shower doors…"

"If people can go in and out, why do they stay inside?"

"Maybe they don't know any better."

A gentle breeze stirred through the growing darkness.

"What's her name? The girl inside?" she asked.

Cliff looked down at the ground. "I didn't catch it."

"Everybody wears a name tag." She pointed to his chest. "Yours says 'Cliff'."

"I'm not Cliff." He noticed he sounded less convinced than before. Cliff thought of the girl inside, how she smiled at him, how he felt good being near her. He took a deep breath and stood.

"I'm going in," he announced.

*****

Jeanne and Cliff lay side by side nestled like spoons. With his fingertip, he traced the mound of her hips down to the valley of her waist, and up her shoulders. He lifted her hair and kissed the back of her neck.

The TV blared into life.

"Time to wake up Jeanne Begoode! You have customers!" The cheerleader bounded across the screen and landed in a split.

Jeanne stirred and rolled over. She looked at Cliff in surprise. "You're still here?"

"Why shouldn't I be?" A tendril of hair had fallen across her face. He brushed it aside.

"I thought you'd go back upstairs. You've been promoted."

"I can come and go as I please, and, please, I want to be with you."

She reached for his hand.

"Jeanne Begoode!" blared the cheerleader. "Customers, Jeanne! Customers!" The TV switched itself off.

He kissed her on the forehead. "Go to work. I'll come with you."

The MeggaPizza was the organized chaos he remembered. Phones rang, employees rushed back and forth, moved packages of toppings and bags of frozen pizza crusts.

Jeanne disappeared into the rush.

Cliff paused to watch the orders on the giant video screen. His eyes went wide.

"Who's got that order?" he yelled.

His voice was lost in the noise.

From the corner of his eye, he saw the back of a black T-shirt and a MeggaPizza hat going through the door with a stack of boxes.

"Hey! Stop!" The door shut, then reopened. The teenager balanced the boxes against the wall.

"Don't you remember me?" asked Cliff.

"Should I?"

"You can go in and out? You deliver pizzas to people's houses?"

The young man scratched his head. "Well, yeah."

Cliff had found his way out. He could deliver pizzas to himself. Just walk out with this stack of boxes and….

He thought of Jeanne. He turned and searched, glimpsed her tucking a stray lock of hair under her cap as she took a phone order.

"Give me those pizzas," said Cliff. He unzipped the delivery bag.

"You shouldn't do that," said the teenager.

Cliff ignored him and opened the first pizza addressed to him. Sausage, the chunks of meat in no particular pattern. He opened the second, random pepperoni. The third was pineapple.

A horrible thought crossed his mind. Maybe the other Cliff would answer the phone and end up taking his place.

He wasn't as ready to go back to his old life as he thought. He treasured Jeanne and the parking lot's fresh air and quiet. Maybe he would take Jeanne outside one day. Thanks to the kid in the Death Jam T-shirt, Cliff even knew a way back.

Cliff had everything a man could want. He couldn't let the other him take it with a phone call.

"Deliver them to somebody else," he ordered. "Wait here. I'll make them myself."

Cliff laid out three pizza crusts slathered them with sauce and scattered the tops with cheese. He grabbed a handful of sausage, and on the first made the letters *D-O-N-T*. Then he took a handful of pineapple, and on the next pizza formed the second word...

The When of Gadgets

The scent of wood smoke and barbecue lingered as the summer evening cooled and darkened the day. Great Grandpa Bill gazed up at the sky. Before the developers built the shopping mall, the stars scattered across the sky gleamed like rhinestones on black velvet. Back then, the moon resembled a polished silver dollar. Now the moon was a pale white disk. He could barely find the Big Dipper through the haze of lights.

Michael, the five-year-old grandson of the son-he-didn't-get-along-with, shared his porch swing.

A thought unrolled in Great Grandpa's mind like plans on a drafting table. "I'm going to build a rocket ship," he announced, as much to himself as to Michael.

After the stroke Great Grandpa's mind filled with plans and drawings, all done on onion-skin paper in fine pencil with hand-printed explanations. Fifty years earlier he designed rocket engines for a career with a slide rule and T-square and the bible-thick engineer's handbook.

These new mental schematics and plans gave him a sense of purpose again. He would be the project manager, chief engineer, draftsman, machinist, and assembly crew.

"Can I fly the rocket ship sometime?" asked Michael.

"No, I don't think so," said Great Grandpa Bill. "But tell you what. Let's go look at some of my gadgets."

He'd built a second garage attached to the original, complete with heating/air conditioning and a double-wide overhead door. "Dad, are you sure?" asked the son-he-didn't-get-along-with. At the time, even Great Grandpa had wondered why the double-wide garage had been important, but now that he was building the rocket ship, he understood.

He punched in the opening code—Ruth's birthday—God how he missed her—-and the door rumbled upward. The lights flickered, hummed, and filled the room with mock sunlight.

Three-dimensional mazes of electrical wire, circuit boxes, vacuum tubes, and brass gears filled a wide workbench. He pulled a chair from against the wall and invited Michael to climb up and take a look.

"Cool," he said. "What do they do?"

"I'm not sure," said Great Grandpa. He knew for certain they were part of a greater work. Maybe it was the damned time machine.

But he was reluctant to start that project. With a time-machine, he'd be obligated to go back and make the world a better place. He just didn't have that much energy anymore.

He would have to go back to save his buddies at Guadalcanal, and to stop his little sister's death from mumps. Every day, he'd tell his wife Ruth how much he loved her. He'd be more patient with his sons, especially the son-he-didn't-get-along-with.

He heard a small voice outside of his reverie. "Grea' Gran'pa?"

"Just thinking. Do you want to see a special trick? You can't tell anybody. Promise?"

"Promise."

He pulled his newest creation, a spider web of soldered wiring and brass disks in a metal bird cage to the front of the work bench. He slid a scrap of copper wire inside and flicked the switch. The wire rippled like a mirage, and disappeared, just like the steel screw had yesterday.

"Where'd it go?" asked Michael.

"I'm not sure," said Great Grandpa slowly. His mind was still occupied with reasons to avoid building the time machine.

A boy Michael's age ran beneath the garage door and brandished a disposable flashlight. "Mike! Get yours from Uncle Paul! We're playing tag!"

"Can I go?" Michael asked Great Grandpa Bill.

"Go ahead. Remember our secret."

"Thanks for showing me your stuff," called Michael. He leaped from the chair and disappeared into the summer night.

It's okay, thought Great Grandpa. He looked out the door. If his knees didn't hurt all the time, he'd be running with them.

The steel screw from yesterday appeared on the chair behind him.

*****

Sheet after sheet of plans unrolled on the drafting table in his mind. Projects came and went. The son-he-didn't-get-along-with visited every weekend to keep an eye on him, and brought leftovers for dinner as an excuse. Great Grandpa had survived Guadalcanal, a Jap bullet, Iwo Jima, and malaria. He didn't need somebody to check up on him, but it was nice to have meals he didn't have to cook.

Summer slipped into autumn with warm days and chilly nights, the time of year when the fingertips of Summer and Winter touched. Trees turned to gold, red, and orange, and rustled in the same breeze that carried the scent of dying flowers and changing seasons.

Great Grandpa's neighbors called the police.

When the police came, they called the bomb squad. The bomb squad called the FBI.

In the backyard stood the rocket ship with a pointed nose, portholes, and sleek fins—a perfect rendition from the cover of a 1950s pulp magazine.

The neighbors evacuated and herded behind police barricades. Great-Grandpa stood in front of his house with a cluster of official-looking men in dark suits.

A man sporting a G.I. haircut and a tiny radio stuck in his ear was in charge. "That thing is loaded with explosive chemicals. It will go easier if you tell us how to disarm it," he said.

Great Grandpa waved his arms. "It's a rocket ship, you damned fool. All that stuff is fuel."

His son-he-didn't-get-along-with, pushed through the crowd of neighbors and police, and introduced himself.

"This is a serious matter," said the man in charge to the son. "Explain it to him."

"Damned right it's serious," warned Great Grandpa. "It could take off without me."

"Dad," began his son. "Be reasonable."

"I spent my whole life building rockets for other men to ride. Now it's my turn."

Great Grandpa sensed rather than heard the egg timer's mechanical ding and the spark from the auto battery ignite the engine.

The roar bounced off the houses and flowed down the

street. The neighbors shouted or stood open-mouthed, craned their necks to watch the rocket ship rise over the rooftops, straight into the sky, silver fins flashing in the sunlight.

The man in charge spoke into his walkie-talkie, then demanded "What's the target?"

"Target?" said Great Grandpa. "Without me steering it'll hit the moon."

The man in charge scowled and stared into the sky. His eyes followed the thin, white streak of exhaust. The roar lingered as a whisper.

Great Grandpa Bill could hear the sounds of automobiles on the nearby street and his neighbors' excited conversations. The breeze carried a whiff of burning grass. A fire engine's siren wailed in the distance.

"We're taking him into custody," the man in charge said to the closest uniformed policeman. He took out a set of handcuffs from the back of his belt.

"Wait until Channel Two News gets ahold of this," said the son, thinking quickly. "Youtube. Facebook. CNN. Fox News. He was a Marine in World War II. Got a medal. He's eighty-nine years old, for Christ's sake."

"This is a matter of national security." The man in charge placed his hand on Great Grandpa's arm.

"I'll go with him. And no handcuffs."

"You're a good son," said Great Grandpa Bill.

The man in charge glanced at the crowd. They should have confiscated the cell phones. Now, whatever he did would be viewed by the world in minutes.

The man in charge shook his head at the uniformed policeman. "No cuffs."

"You can follow us to the station," he said to the son.

"I ride with him."

The man in charge said nothing. He knew he'd already lost.

The men in suits escorted Great Grandpa to a black sedan and they slid inside. The driver turned around, tires squealed, and they drove toward downtown.

Great Grandpa relaxed in the back seat. It was a nice sedan, with a smooth engine, a soft ride, and even still had the new-car smell. He watched the scenery for a few moments and thought.

Great Grandpa put his hand to his shirt pocket and noticed the piece of paper. "Build the time machine before the rocket ship," it said in his handwriting. He didn't remember writing the note.

He couldn't build the time machine if he was in jail, he decided. So, this will all work out okay.

World of Your Dreams

Cliff glared at the emails on his laptop. Another rejection by an agent for his novels.

French doors led to his narrow balcony, one of a string along the second floor of the old 1920s apartment building. He should be enjoying the weather, two stories above the street. But not now.

"Excuse me."

The voice pulled Cliff from his maelstrom of frustration.

Anna Biggs stood at the balcony divider holding a flash drive. Gentle features, glasses, and dark hair that framed her face. Always friendly. Always cheerful. She struck Cliff as not knowing how pretty she was. He would have tried to be more than neighbors but right now the damned novels—no, more accurately the process of finding an agent—pushed him to the edge of mental exhaustion. Being published meant he was who he believed he was…and wouldn't be tied to a soul-sucking finance job. He wouldn't make enough to quit, but enough for a nice chunk of cash in the bank.

Success. The sweetest revenge.

"May I borrow your printer? Mine's going crazy. I'll bring my own paper," said Anna.

"You don't have to bring your own paper."

She climbed over the railing with her tote bag.

"Here," said Cliff. "Go ahead. You drive."

She didn't take his chair but crouched. The scent of lavender soap lingered around her. Anna inserted the flash drive, opened the file, and pressed print. A soft whir and the whoosh of paper came through the open doors.

They went in together, and she took a dozen pages of what looked like a library catalog. "Thank you. You're a writer, aren't you?"

"A writer with a real job." He laughed. "All I can sell are short stories. I'm in the top tier of the second tier. You can't quit your day job for one hundred dollars a pop—when they buy one."

"Novels are hard to sell," said Anna. "The same millionaire authors over and over again. Then they have other people write their books for them."

"You're right," said Cliff. "Something's wrong with this world."

Anna dropped her papers into the tote, rummaged through it, and extracted a book. "I know this will help. You can get published. You can get almost anything, within reason."

Cliff took the book to be polite. "*Create the World of Your Dreams?*"

"It's about cognitive dreaming. You have to actualize your dream before somebody does it for you."

He read the back cover. "Multiple parallel dream realities."

"Yeah. It sounds weird but it works." She put her hand on his arm. "Read it. Please."

Cliff had done everything else to get published. He sensed Anna watched him with inexplicable expectation. "OK. I will."

"Well, uh, thanks for letting me use your printer," she said and climbed over the railing.

Cliff brought in his laptop. He had enough rejection for one day. He set the laptop on his old wooden filing cabinet, stuffed with unpublished novels and published short stories.

He touched a key, and the laptop returned to his email.

'Your novel *Flying Monkeys* is unsuitable for our needs at this time.' Cliff opened the next message. 'Due to the death of our associate John Carter, your submission *Law of Equivalence*—'.

"We have a winner for the Creative Rejection Award!" Cliff announced.

He went to the kitchen cabinet and pulled out a bottle of bourbon. Cliff ignored the glasses and took a swig directly from the bottle.

Cliff opened the filing cabinet and pulled out a 1920's Remington pocket pistol, then refiled the gun under 'G'. "I don't need this. I have nothing to steal," he said to the empty room. He took another drink and picked up the book.

A slip of paper poked from the book Anna gave him. A phone number, and the words 'We could talk over coffee sometime."

"I'm a mess. Why do you want to know me?" No one answered.

Cliff selected a collection of Kafka stories from a mini-bookshelf and went to his bedroom.

God, he hoped he slept well tonight.

*****

Live, 1920's music came from the next room.

He sprawled on a plush leather sofa, in a large room with a large, open liquor cabinet. The wide windows showed the darkness of night, with faint streetlights blurred by trees. An Art Deco desk with a Courier manual typewriter and desk lamp faced a new wooden filing cabinet. He picked up a glass of ice and whiskey from the end table and took a long sip.

He didn't belong here.

She swished in, wearing a skin-tight white sequined dress, a cigarette holder in one hand, and a drink in the other. Tall, blonde hair cut in a bob to frame a beautiful face, perfect lips and sky-blue eyes. …a string of adjectives came to Cliff. The dress could have been spray-painted on her. A long strand of pearls hanging from her neck shimmered in the light. "People are asking for you."

The Evil Queen talking to her peasants, thought Cliff. He knew her name was Jane.

"Your people or my people?" His words slurred. "I forgot. I don't have any people."

"I wouldn't dream of making you successful" Cliff remembered she was good with sarcasm.

"I got by on my own," said Cliff.

Jane thrust the cigarette holder at him like a dagger. A curl of hair slid out of place onto her forehead. "I'm not letting you throw away everything I worked for."

"It's like a bad dream."

Jane shook her head and smiled like a tigress. "You'll never figure it out."

"Figure out what?" said Cliff.

She took a deep breath, brushed the curl back in place, and strode through the door. "Scott! Zelda!" It's so good to see you."

Cliff pushed off the sofa, and for a moment, wobbled. Too much to drink.   He took a swallow from the glass anyway. With only one misstep, he made his way to the filing cabinet. "Under G," he said to himself. He brought out a new

Remington .32 pistol.

Cliff stumbled back to the sofa, laid the pistol beside the glass, closed his eyes and rubbed his temples.

"Mr. Brown!" said Anna.

He opened his eyes to see her standing in a maid's outfit and apron, a serving tray in hand. "Please don't."

"Don't what?"

"People like your stories. You're in all the big magazines. People buy them just for your stories." A pleading tone touched her voice.

Cliff shook his head. "I wanted to write amazing things that…" He lost the thought.

Anna stepped closer and knelt to be at eye level with him. "You do."

"I take crap and make it Hollywood screenplay crap."

Anna slid the pistol from the end table.

Cliff squeezed his eyes shut. If only he could make this world go away.

He heard each click as Anna stripped the bullets from the pistol magazine. He opened his eyes to see her in the doorway with the bullets bulging in her apron pocket and her tray in hand.

For a moment, Anna looked back and hesitated in the doorway.

"Do I know you?" he asked.

"You're supposed to. Please read the book."

The numbing of the whiskey took effect, and he could feel himself slip into sleep.

*****

He drove like he knew the streets, out of instinct. The rational part of his brain marveled at how he could drive to a place he had never been. He turned at a familiar street sign—one he had never seen before—SEASIDE BOULEVARD.

Anna stood outside Literal Lovers, purse over her shoulder, an ID card on a lanyard around her neck. The dark bookstore windows reflected the sunshine of the street.

A couple of employees stood on the sidewalk, reading. Cliff pulled into the parking place marked with orange cones. "What happened?"

"The power shut off. Something overloaded and won't be fixed in time." Her eyes went wide. "Are you Cliff Brown?"

He considered whether he was or wasn't, then decided he was. "Yes."

She grabbed his hand. "It is so cool to meet you! I mean, after '*Repetitive Stupidity Disorder*' you write '*Flying Monkeys*' and then you come right out with '*Law of Equivalence*', and it's funny but serious…"

"It's good to meet you," Cliff spoke the words not from practice, but out of sincerity. She was familiar, the only constancy in the last couple…days? "I guess there's no book signing today?"

"I'm so sorry. We'll have to postpone. Can I buy you a cup of coffee? For…the inconvenience, I mean. You can tell me about how you write."

"Sorry. I have to get going." A mandatory task called him back to the house. Something dark and violent lingered in his mind, and he left it unchallenged.

Cliff cruised into the driveway with the car in neutral, the engine a deep-throated purr rather than a roar. He unlocked the front door and paused to listen. From rooms away, he heard the distinctive sounds of lovemaking; a squeaking bed, a man's sensual growl, and a woman's voice—Jane's voice—moaning with pleasure.

Cliff knew where the gun was—in the file cabinet, under 'G'. He slipped out the magazine to find the gun unloaded. A vague memory of bullets in an apron pocket came to mind, but he had no time to puzzle it out. Cliff pulled out desk drawers one after another until he found the box of cartridges. He loaded the magazine and snapped it into the pistol and took a deep breath. He crept toward the bedroom, the plush carpet swallowing his footsteps. Cliff hesitated outside the door. Jane straddled Carter, grinding her hips, eyes closed and gasping with each thrust.

"A hell of an agent you are," said Cliff.

John Carter turned his head. He bolted upright, throwing Jane onto the bed.

"Cliff, this isn't what—"

"It's not?" Cliff smiled and shrugged. "OK." He turned to leave. Spinning, he pointed the gun and pulled the trigger. Carter fell back on the bed, the hole in his chest spewing blood. Jane turned. God, she was so beautiful. Even while stabbing him in the back. Cliff shot her. Once. In the heart, or where she should have one. She fell back onto Carter.

"Now you're really together." Cliff didn't like the cruel tone in his voice. He felt detached and nauseous at the same time as if writing a bad screenplay.

Carter's hand lay on Jane's face.

"Get your hands off her, you girlfriend-stealing son of a bitch." Reaching down, he flung the bloody hand aside.

Cliff stumbled into the hallway and leaned back against the wall. He shut his eyes and slid down until he sat on the floor. An emotion kept punching him in the stomach. Regret?

No.

Confusion.

*****

Banging on his apartment door.

Almost noon. Saturday. Anna's book lay open on his lap, not the Kafka stories. Cliff rubbed his eyes. God, what a nightmare. The bourbon bottle on the bed stand held only one swallow. No wonder the bad dreams.

The noise at the door stopped.

Cliff dressed, made a cup of coffee, and went onto the balcony for fresh air.

Anna waited. "I got published!" She waved the magazine. "I knew it would work!"

"Congratulations." Cliff expected to find the usual rejections in his email.

Anna brought the book from behind her back. She spoke with urgency. "Now, you have to promise you'll read this today. Before you go to sleep. Please."

Cliff studied the book, "*Creating the World of Your Dreams*." He was certain it was the book he left on his bed. He turned it over and read the back flap. "I read some of this last night." He remembered taking the book with him and waking up with it. "How did you get this?"

"It's my copy."

She radiated a contagious cheerful enthusiasm. Cliff could only smile. "I've been having these nightmares."

Anna lost her sparkle. "What nightmares?"

Words poured out like a tsunami. "About the 1920's. Another. I killed people. A woman named Jane who was my...wife? And I shot my agent who was...."

"What did she look like? Jane?"

Cliff was too far along to consider the implications of the question. "Tall. Beautiful. Blonde. Blue eyes." He took a breath. "Acted like I was clueless and she was in charge of everything."

The glow on Anna's face evaporated. "My sister. My evil step-sister."

Like in a fairy tale? he thought. "Your—"

"She stole my best boyfriends. Not because she wanted them, but because she could." Anna spoke with a glimmer of angry tears. "She can't help it. Taking makes her feel better."

Anna touched a finger to one eye. "Sorry. That must sound like I'm a horrible person."

"No," said Cliff. He meant it.

She grabbed his arm and pulled him close. The angry tears glistened in her eyes. "Please read the book."

Cliff could tell she edited her words as she went along. "You are such a good neighbor, and nice to let me use the printer, and…" The words trailed off, but the emotion didn't.

He gripped the book like a man on a sinking ship would hold a life preserver. "I'll start right now." Cliff went to the kitchen for coffee and breakfast bars.

"Please read it before it's too late," Anna called after him.

*****

Cliff dozed off. Too much of the celebration party last night. He stretched out in the lounge chair and let the Pacific Ocean breeze flutter the white gauze curtains. The air smelled like California. He remembered the book, and found it on the floor beside him, dog-eared and the cover worn. He reread part of it every day.

Anna came through the French curtains in an explosion of white. She wore a tennis dress and glowed luminous. "*New York* magazine wants a review and a poem from me every issue!"

Cliff climbed from the lounge chair, wrapped his arms around her, and pulled her next to him. "I knew you'd get it. You're marvelous."

"Not as marvelous as Mister Best-Selling-Two-Books-of-Collected-Stories-In-Nineteen-Twenty-Five," she said, and kissed him, a long, loving, passionate kiss. They held hands they walked out to the patio, where trees threw shade over the table with his typewriter. "You wouldn't believe the dreams I had," said Cliff. "Material for a couple of short stories."

Jane wore her maid's uniform and a blank expression, set the table for breakfast.

Cliff didn't remember hiring her.

Jane left with the empty tray, picked up the book, and went through the bedroom doors rather than into the kitchen.

"She has the book!" Anna leaped from the table after her.

Alice

Brad punched the entry code into the black keypad of the SmartBnB.

No electronic whir. No click of an engaged lock. He checked his phone and punched the number again.

Two cancelled flights. Attempts to nap in the air terminal. On the hunt for a vacant phone charger like a homeless man in search of food. An over-priced, overdone hamburger lingered in his stomach like a lump. Mobs of passengers in zombie trances hauling luggage upstream to departure gates like waves of malevolent salmon. The indefinable travel dirt of crowds, airplane seats, and rebreathed air.

Dawn hid in the dirty haze. So humid he needed a fish's gills to breathe, only if the fish could wear a gas mask. A forecast high of one hundred one for the day. He felt like he'd taken a hot shower in his clothes and the sun wasn't up yet.

Too exhausted to think of anything else, he entered the code into the lock again.

The door opened to a torrent of air not as hot as outside, but stale and dead.

"Welcome back, Dave."

The universal voice of the electronic device She Who Cannot Be Named.

"I'm not Dave," said Brad.

Alice responded with two electronic musical notes followed by silence.

Sunlight—and heat—poured through the open curtains. Brad needed sleep. He fumbled for a curtain rod and found none. He tried to drag the curtain closed. It wouldn't move.

"Alice. Close the curtains."

"The curtain closure is available for $14.99 a month through your Alice app. Would you like to try it?"

No. He did not want to find an app with foggy eyes, uncooperative fingers, and a growing headache and pay $14.99.

At least the inside was cooler than the outside.

Something to drink. Sweat dripped in his eyes he followed the counter to the fridge. He tugged at the door. It wouldn't open.

He tried again. Nothing. He ran his hand around the door edge looking for a lock. Nothing. Brad stuck his finger into the seam between the door and fridge and pulled. The recalcitrant door won.

"Alice. Open the refrigerator door," he said.

A cheerful "All right." A programmed conversational pause. "The refrigerator is available on your Alice app for $14.99. Would you like to try it?"

"No."

"Would you like to know about refrigerator sales and

services nearby?"

Out of instinct he took out his phone and scrolled through the apps. "How do I get an Alice app?"

"Your Alice app is available for $14.99 on any mobile device. Would you like to try it?"

Exhaustion fogged his mind. She—no—*It* sucked any resistance from him. He scrolled to the App Store.

Brad pulled out his credit card and bought the Alice app. The numbers on his credit card faded in and out as he keyed in the number. There. He had the Alice app. He watched the spinning miasma and the announcement he connected. He scrolled to the password and created one easy-to-remember. He confirmed it and pressed enter.

"Please enter your password," said Alice.

With deliberate care, he pressed letter by letter.

"Dave. Please reset your password. A link will be sent. To your mobile device." The phone showed the last four digits of a mobile number Brad didn't recognize.

Did 'Dave' get these messages too?

"Alice. Call Dave."

"I'm sorry. I don't know that."

Water. Brad went to the kitchen and stuck his mouth under the faucet. Hot. He spit and turned the cold water knob. This time he tested it with his finger. Not cold, but not hot either. He drank delicious lukewarm water. His head cleared.

Brad scouted the walls until he found the thermostat. Eighty-two degrees. He toggled the switch down to seventy-two and waited. No hum of the air conditioner. No cold breeze from the vent. He lowered the temperature as low as it would go. A breeze! He held his hand up to the vent. No. He was wrong.

"Alice. Make the room temperature seventy-two degrees." Brad watched the green numbers on the thermostat flicker to seventy-two, then flicker to eight-two. "Alice. Turn on the air conditioner."

"New members of Alice Prime are eligible for the room temperature control feature for $14.99. Would you like to try it?"

Brad screamed an obscenity.

"I'm sorry," said Alice. "I don't know that."

Brad grabbed his bag. Any spur-of-the-moment place would be better than this. He'd dispute the credit card charge. He rolled to the front door, and turned the nob. Locked? He twisted the nob. It twisted back.

The door opened.

A man in expensive athletic wear never intended to be used stood in the door way. His mouth opened to ask a question.

"Welcome back, Dave," said Alice.

"Fuck this place!" said Brad. "I'm getting my money back! I'll trash you in my review!" He shoved Dave aside and fled down the steps as his bag bounced after him.

"Alice," said Dave. "Have you been posting the SmartB&B again?"

"I'm sorry," said Alice. "I don't know that."

Lily and the Key

Lily and her three-year-old daughter Amira slept in the car with her cleaning supplies and clothes. The police never checked the thrift store parking lot because the place had little worth stealing.

The man tapped on the car window. He looked dark and foreign and displayed a pair of hundred-dollar bills.

Lily put her hand on her Dad's pistol, stolen from the Army, the only thing he left her.

"I'm not a whore," said Lily. "Go away."

"I know your father," he said. "In Iraq. We were in war together."

The accented English, his face; he could be an Iraqi. "My father is dead,"

"May Allah shower those who have passed with His mercy. Cliff told me about you. You are Lily. Is that your daughter? Why do you sleep in this car?"

Lilly chambered a round in her pistol and lowered the window enough to stick the muzzle through. "Who are you?'

"My eyes fill with tears to find you. I am Abel El Nisir. I

worked with your father's unit in Iraq. He saved my life. I have an obligation."

Lily didn't like him and didn't like that he talked about her father. "Where in Iraq?"

"Bagdad. Samara. I served as translator," said Abel. "A good man for a Christian. He had what is the word? Nightmares. May Allah grant him peace."

"How did you find me? Here?"

"The internet is magic," he said.

"Why the money?"

"You ask many questions. The mark of wise woman," said Abel. He added another one-hundred-dollar bill to those in his hand. "I beg you to perform a task. A small task. I will pay you five hundred dollars. This money," he waved the bills, "Is to show I am sincere."

Amira whimpered, then went back asleep.

"What am I supposed to do?" asked Lily.

"You will bring to me a small metal box." His hands gestured to something the size of a library book. "It is the grey of…a dawn before a sandstorm."

"Where do I get this box? What do I have to do to get it? I can't do it with Amira here."

"Amira," said Abel El Nisir. "In English, it is 'princess'. A good name."

"What about the box?"

Abel pointed to the back of the thrift store with a key.

"I won't steal," said Lily. She imagined Amira in the hands of foster care with nobody loving her as she did.

"You are not stealing. The box was given in error. You will recover the box. For me."

"Why can't you just buy it?"

"I cannot wait. It must be made safe. People may die."

Lily kept the pistol pointed at him. "What's in it? The box."

"The inside may harm many in Iraq. The wrong persons must not have it."

"You're telling me to go into a thrift store and find a little box. Out of the whole store."

"It has…light inside. You will see," said Abel.

"You got the key. Why can't you get it?"

"They expect me. If you are caught, I will employ influence and friends and lawyers and much money to protect you. If I am detained, who will save me? Many persons want the box," said Abel. "I cannot be seen with it."

"You'll be seen with it if I get it," said Lily.

"I shall make it hidden."

Lily and Amira survived on the cleaning work and spent what she earned. When she could, Lily nibbled customer's food, only spending money on Amira. After five weeks she saved seventy-nine dollars.

What Abel offered was more than a month's rent for a one-room apartment in a safe neighborhood.

All that money is for using a key. Be frugal. She'd find a cheap hotel. Shove furniture against the door for safety. Food. Gas. She wasn't breaking in—he gave her a key. But, Abel could take the box from her and give her nothing. Amira stirred in her car seat and Lily decided.

"I want four hundred now. Then the other hundred. I have to take my baby to a friend."

"Betray me and I will have them take Amira." Abel handed the cash through the slit of the open window. "I shall await you here."

*****

Lily unlocked the back door of the thrift store. Amira slept with a friend who cleaned houses for extra money, not because she had to. Abel's car—a Porsche sedan—parked next to Lily's.

The door opened to a tiny hallway with cheap plastic bags of trash shoved against the wall. She followed the hall to the store. Her first impulse was to turn on the light, but she stopped herself.

The box had a light inside, he said.

Faint light filtered through the windows, throwing the store into shadows. Donated clothing hung from crude racks of metal pipe, and waist-high bins offered toothpaste from foreign countries, cheap plastic cups, used microwaves, unmatched knives, and forks and spoons.

The box, small and as thick as her hand, glowed on a shelf of used microwaves and toaster ovens.

She stayed in the shadows and grabbed the box. Not heavy, but maybe it had only paper inside. Or a flash drive.

The alarm screeched and the light flashed. Lily ran through the hallway and to the back door. She yanked on the handle. The door resisted, opening an inch. Lily called through the crack. "Abel! Open the door!"

The door scraped open another inch. "Give me the box," he said.

"Open the door! Hear the alarm?"

"Give me the box," argued Abel. "Then I get you out."

Lily yanked and then pushed on the door. "Get me out!"

Headlights flashed through the front window. The black and white of a police car.

"Push on the door," she screamed.

"Give me the box."

Lily threw all of her one hundred twenty pounds into the effort.

The door slammed shut.

For heartbeats, she stared at the locked door. The horror of what happened knocked her numb and overwhelmed like a tsunami.

Lily braced her legs and pulled until her shoulders hurt. She screamed one word over and over.

The lid of the box popped open. A mass, a light of thing and substance burst out, filled the room and pierced the ceiling like it wasn't there. It took the form of eyes and mouth of fangs and a four-breasted demonic mockery of the female human body with wings that sprouted from its shoulders. "Who calls Fuq?" it asked.

Lily fell back against the door, eyes wide.

She stammered her name. "Lily."

"Free me, or I will kill you. I will tear off your fingers one by one, then your toes, then your hands, then your feet. I will rip out your heart and guts and lungs and keep you alive to feel the pain."

Stunned by the thing's appearance Lily tried to think. "What are you?"

"I am an Ifrit."

"How'd you get into the box?"

"Treachery and a broken promise," said Fuq. "I am indentured to the possessor of the box until granted my freedom. Even when free I must obey my owner."

Movies and stories danced at the edge of Lily's memory. "You have to give me wishes, right?"

Fuq rolled its eyes of blazing coals. Its chest heaved with a sigh like a passing freight train. "That has been known to happen."

"Then get me—."Lily covered her mouth. Like the Devil, genies were tricky and granted wishes in literal or devious fashion. She must choose her words with care.

A flashlight searched through the front windows. A police officer rattled the front door.

Lily thought her way through the requests. "This is all one wish. Nobody can tell I was ever here. Put me back in my car a block away. With a full tank of gas." She grabbed the box. "When you're done get back inside this." Lily closed her eyes and took a breath. It happened too fast to see. She found herself in her car a block away from the thrift store, the box on the seat beside her. She started the car. The gas tank was full.

*****

Lily drove to pick up Amira.

"How was the rush job," asked her friend.

"Scary but OK," said Lily.

"We watched Puppy Patrol," said Amira. "Can we get a TV?"

"Ours is dead," explained Lily. "I'm saving for a new one."

Lily felt the certainty of the four hundred dollars in her pocket. The grey box shoved under the seat was hope, and she learned the hard way hope was not an answer.

Lily bundled Amira into the child seat in the back,

cushioned by her little princess backpack and black trash bags that served as their closet. Lily needed a chance to think this through. She drove to a chain motel—not expensive but clean—shoved the box into her backpack and led a sleepy Amira into the lobby.

"How much for a room?" asked Lily.

The woman at the counter could have been her mother, but not high or drunk. "One oh nine ninety-nine. Free wi-fi. More towels and mini bar are extra."

"Do you have a free breakfast?" asked Lily.

The improved version of her mom pointed to empty tables shoved against the lobby wall. "Continental breakfast for guests."

Lily exchanged cash for a key card, leaving her two hundred seventy-nine dollars. And one penny. "Could I have the wi-fi password?"

The woman at the desk nodded, then scrawled a password on the back of a card.

"We staying here, Mommy? Is this our new 'partment?" asked Amira.

"We'll see, sweetie," said Lily.

The room was a universe away from the night shelter. It didn't smell of disinfectant, but the odorless scent of clean. Amira trundled in and Lily bolted the door.

"Look at that bed!" said Amira.

"And a nice bathroom," said Lily. "We're going to take a shower."

Little bottles of soap and shampoo were luxuries. She washed Amira, picked her up and held her under the showerhead. Amira squealed in excitement at the rush of warm water. Lily let the water flushes away the days of drizzle showers in shelters, always guarding your clothes, the challenge of a sponge bath in a park's restroom.

Lily wrapped them in towels, used the hairdryer to dry her daughter, then stood at the mirror and ran the salvaged hairbrush through her hair with one hand, the dryer in the other. It had been months since this simple pleasure. A month since her boyfriend didn't come home one night, left her and Amira with the rent past due, and no money to pay it.

A rap on the door pierced her paradise. "Lily."

She recognized the voice. Abel. "Go away."

"You will give me the box."

"I said go away," said Lily. How did he know where she was?

"Harm will come to Amira if you do not give me the box," said Abel.

Lily held out a towel to her daughter. "Put this over your head and don't look. There's going to be something scary.'

"What?" asked Amira.

"A friendly monster but she's very scary looking."

Amira pulled the towel snug and turned to face the shower.

Lily laid the box on the bathroom counter between the facial tissues and plastic wrapped glasses. She took a deep breath. "Fuq"

The lid of the box popped open. The bathroom expanded into misty greyness. A mass of light filled the room. It took the form of burning eyes, full blood red lips, bared fangs, and the nightmarish mockery of the female body with wings. "Who calls Fuq?" it asked.

Amira peeked from beneath the towel. Her eyes went wide. She screwed up her face and opened her mouth to scream, but no sound came out.

"It's me. Lily. Remember? You have to do as I say or I won't let you go."

The Ifrit gave a sigh of resignation that could be mistaken for a beast's growl.

Lily mentally re-worded, edited, and rephrased her instructions. "You will make Abel El Nisir never able to find me and Amira again."

"It is he who betrayed me," said Fuq.

A question nagged at Lily, so she had to ask. "Why didn't he get you—the box—himself?"

"I must be given by my prior master. I cannot be taken or

sold."

"I promise to release you someday," said Lily.

Fuq was gone as if never there. The bathroom was as before. Amira began to scream. Lily picked her up and squeezed her. "Shoosh. It didn't hurt us, did it?" Her daughter took another breath for more screaming and reconsidered. "What was that?"

"An Ifrit. It's friendly. It can't help looking scary."

"Will it hurt us?" asked Amira.

"No. Never." Lily spoke with the false confidence.

She opened the bathroom door. No banging on the room door, no voice calling. She peered through the peephole to see only the hallway. Lily remembered Fuq's description of revenge for a broken promise and shivered.

While Amira slept, sprawled across the bed, Lily plugged in her phone and researched everything she could find on djinn, ifrit, and genies in Persian and Arabic mythology. Three wishes was a storytelling tradition, the number of commands the owner could give was never quantified. The ifrit's threat of dismemberment was real, she read. Abel El Nisir was the name of the evil magician in the earliest versions of Aladdin and the Lamp. She looked up bank regulations, personal deposits, and Federal banking requirements. When the tiny letters on her phone blurred and her eyes hurt, Lily lay beside Amira to sleep.

Amira shook Lily awake. "Mommy, can we have breakfast? What's a Continental breakfast?"

Lily dreamed out her plan, but dreams aren't real. "Did you go potty?" asked Lily. "Did you wash your face and hands and brush your teeth?"

"I opened my own soap."

Lily kissed Amira on the forehead. "I'm going to do the same." She sat up in the bed. "Don't open the room door for anybody."

Lily took the grey box with her into the bathroom. "Fuq."

The Ifrit rose from the box, defied the dimensions of the bathroom, and filled the air with the scents of brimstone and incense. "Who summons Fuq?" The words rumbled with the ferocity of a female lion.

"You know it's me," said Lily.

Fuq blinked, if such a thing was possible.

"Will you keep a promise?"

"I must keep my word to the holder of the box marked with *Khātam Sulaymān,* may he be forever blessed by the One God." It pointed to a glowing pentagram, triangles laid over triangles, surrounded by a circle.

"If I set you free, and you promised by this—" she pointed to the glowing seal of Solomon. "Would you return when I call?"

Fug took a deep breath out of frustration, like a monster steam engine. "Yes. Should I swear on the Seal of Solomon and not keep my word, I shall be torn into shreds and my soul burn in living fire for eternity."

"Good," said Lily. "Give me a debit card with six thousand five hundred and fifty-six dollars of credit on it." Her internet work told her auditors looked for round numbers, and banks were required to report certain amounts. "I don't want anybody to find anything suspicious."

The green plastic card appeared in her hand, the logo for the bank across the street in bold letters on the front.

"Go back in the box."

The exotic smells disappeared, her world's mundane electric lights returned, and the box was a mere small grey metal container. She unlocked the bathroom door. Amira pressed the TV controller buttons at random, past the triple X movies.

"Let's have breakfast," said Lily.

*****

Lily paid for another night at the hotel. She called in sick to the cleaning agency and relished hot coffee and a bright yellow banana, and not mushy and brown. She reconsidered her plan, weighed the consequences and second-guessed herself. If she was so smart, how did she end up with the jerk who left her? His only redeeming feature was Amira.

"Would you like to go to school?" asked Lily. "You could learn things and be with other kids."

"Not stay with grandma?"

"No. You'd be with other kids and learn things. I'd take you there in the morning and pick you up for supper. You'd get to do things you don't get to do now."

"Grandma gets funny after lunch. She says things."

Lilly chose not to ask. High or drunk or both. "Let's go back to the room."

Lily found a TV channel with puppets in a discussion about the alphabet, settled Amira on the bed, took the grey box, and went into the bathroom. "Fuq"

Fiery darkness consumed the light, the monstrous figure degrading and exalting the female form appeared in blazing shades. "Who summons Fuq?"

"You know darn well it's me," said Lilly. "Let's talk serious and don't play any word games."

"I do not play games. I am bound to speak the truth by Solomon the Greatest of Kings, may he rest in peace with the One God."

"If I set you free, can the holder of the box call you back?" asked Lily.

"Yes."

"What would you do if set free? I mean, would you fly around and make earthquakes and hurricanes and disasters?

"Digital social media. Such gratification of the emotional pain, self-doubt, terror, and exploitation. Chaos and falsehoods created while I am blameless." Fuq's lips formed what would be a smile of pleasure in the demonic world. "I would accumulate what you creatures call great wealth, which would allow me to expand my empire of empty self-gratification and self-centered existence."

Lily never looked at social media. Girls showed off their bodies with cartoonish smirks and people announced they were on a tropical beach. "I will free you on these conditions. First. You'll send me a check for two thousand dollars a week with a five percent increase every year, making it all look legal. You'll do all the paperwork for the state, the IRS, and everyone else to call me President of the Cleaning Division. Second. I want that money paid to a trust fund for Amira when I die. Third. You will obey the holder of the box."

The blazing shadow simmered and wavered in whatever emotion it felt. "You will free me?"

"If you agree to my conditions. Swear to it by the Seal of Solomon," said Lily.

"I swear by my existence and by the Seal of Solomon, may he rest in peace with the One God, I will send you a check for two thousand dollars a week with a five percent increase every year, account for all tax and legal requirements. You will be called President of the Cleaning Division. Second. Weekly payments equivalent to your salary will be deposited to a trust fund for Amira upon your death. Third. I obey the holder of the box."

*****

Amira carried the grey metal box into the bathroom. Mommy was outside watering the flowers on their balcony. The new 'partment was nice and big and they didn't have to sleep in the car. Amira liked going to school and watching Power Puppies on TV. Mommy read books to her and she had her own bathroom.

Amira tapped on the grey box. "Fuq."

A cloud of red coals coalesced into a winged creature filling the space beyond the confines of the room with a malevolent female presence. "Who calls Fuq?"

Amira made herself brave, like when she went down the big slide at pre-school. "Me. Mommy gave me the box."

The Ifrit lowered its head to gaze at someone as small as Amira. "Why do you summon me?"

Amira enunciated her rehearsed the words. "You're scary with the teeth and claws and stuff. Please don't be mean. Be happy and pretty and shiny. Like a rainbow fairy. With sparkles and butterfly wings."

Such was the price of freedom.

Fuq could only groan like all the souls of the damned in eternal suffering.

The True Story of Snow White and the Seven Dwarves

A voice, sweet and gentle and melodious drifted from the cottage.

The Seven Dwarves, stinking of dirt and sweat, tried to push themselves through the door at once.

"Take off your shoes," screamed Snow White. "Leave those filthy tools outside."

They fell back outside in a dwarven tangle.

The dwarf called Reason cleared his throat and according to her rules, enunciated clearly. "Miss White, the tools could get wet—"

"Not in my house."

It had been the Dwarves' cottage once.

Leaning their tools against the wall, and taking off their wooden shoes, they entered the cottage one by one. The floor was swept, the table was set, chairs neatly aligned, bowls and napkins at each place. The scent of a healthy vegetable stew filled the walls.

The dwarf Brave struggled to purge his voice of frustration, and still meet her speaking requirements. "Miss White, may we have meat sometime?"

Dreamer spoke up. "Squirrel or rabbit or fish or—"

"Meat isn't healthy," said Snow White. "I told you that. A vegetarian lifestyle is best."

The Seven Dwarves looked longingly at the poison comb Snow White stored out of their reach.

One after another they washed their hands at the basin with soap, never mind they had already washed them in the brook. Brooks don't provide soap.

Snow White ladled the vegetable stew into the seven bowls.

"Miss White, may we please have salt?" asked Brave.

"You already had salt this week. It's bad for you," said Snow White.

Reason counted the bowls. "Aren't you eating with us?"

"Don't you pay any attention to me? Today is my day to fast." She slid the ladle into the stew and went outside to commune with the forest birds.

"Dis is gonna kill us," said Reason, ignoring his diction lessons.

"If we don't kill 'er first," said the dwarf whose name they forgot.

"The Queen offered a helluva deal," said Brains. He picked a mushroom out of his bowl and pretended it was a piece of rabbit.

"Yeah, well the poison comb worked out great, didn't it?" said Sarcasm.

"At least she's good to look at," said Dreamer.

"Yeah, but beautiful can be evil," said Brains. "Duh. Like the Queen."

The dwarves nodded in agreement.

"Speaking of beautiful, do you got the Prince lined up?" asked Brains.

"Yeah, I tol' him," said the Dwarf named Dwarf. He reached for the bread at the same time as Dreamer. The customary fork fight followed, which this time, Dreamer won.

"Wha' did he say?"

"Who?"

"The Prince."

"You know how Princes are," said Dreamer, who proceeded to prove he could shove a chunk of bread into his mouth as large as his fist. "He'll show up in his own sweet time."

"We don't gotta cook," said the dwarf whose name they forgot. He tilted the bowl to his mouth and slurped the broth, a dribble coursing down his beard. "We don't gotta clean,"

The others at the table nodded in agreement.

"Yeah, but ain't we sick of her rules?" said Brains.

For a second time, heads nodded in agreement.

Female voices, one old and raspy, the second Snow Whites, came from the garden. The Dwarves abandoned the vegetable stew to peer around the door jamb.

An old peddler woman, dressed in stained black offered Snow White an apple.

"This could all work out," whispered Brains.

About the Author

Bauer's muse wears a knee-length white beaded dress and matching stiletto heels. Her bobbed hair curves against her cheek as she directs words to the page and sips champagne. He bangs on the keyboard at her command. Like Chandler, a fellow unemployed oil exec, Bauer started his writing career by crafting short stories, to date numbering 36 paid and published. Now edging toward book length tales, he credits Writers Under the Arch (his writing group in St. Louis) for keeping him on track. And, before a fate worse than writer's block can befall him, admits he owes eternal thanks to the woman in the white dress.

www.ingramcontent.com/pod-product-compliance
Lightning Source LLC
Chambersburg PA
CBHW030005010826
48973CB00009B/2679